Castles in t

A Wargame of Flying Battleships

By Eric Farrington

OSPREY GAMES
Bloomsbury Publishing Plc
Kemp House, Chawley Park, Cumnor Hill, Oxford OX2 9PH, UK
29 Earlsfort Terrace, Dublin 2, Ireland
1385 Broadway, 5th Floor, New York, NY 10018, USA
E-mail: info@ospreygames.co.uk
www.ospreygames.co.uk

OSPREY GAMES is a trademark of Osprey Publishing Ltd

First published in Great Britain in 2022

A catalog record for this book is available from the British Library.

ISBN: PB 9781472844965; eBook 9781472844934; ePDF 9781472844941;
XML 9781472844958
 22 23 24 25 26 10 9 8 7 6 5 4 3 2 1

Typeset by PDQ Digital Media Solutions, Bungay, UK
Printed in India by Replika Press Pvt. Ltd.

Osprey Games supports the Woodland Trust, the UK's leading woodland
conservation charity.

To find out more about our authors and books visit www.ospreypublishing.com.
Here you will find extracts, author interviews, details of forthcoming events and
the option to sign up for our newsletter.

Photographs

All photographs courtesy of Brigade Models and the miniatures from their
Imperial Skies range. Their website can be found at
http://www.brigademodels.co.uk/

Contents

The World After the Martians

The Martian Invasion of 1872 was a horrific event that changed the course of world events in terrible and unforeseen ways. Despite the gallant efforts of Great Britain's military, it was not the war machines of man that put a stop to the invasion, but rather the microbes of Earth. The great Martian war machines remained where they fell.

It was only a matter of time before the fantastic and new alien technological remnants allowed mankind to achieve great scientific discoveries. Great Britain was the first to profit from such advances. They soon spread across the world by the power of commerce, telegraph, and undersea cable.

Research into the advanced Martian war machines led to one of the most innovative and groundbreaking discoveries of the day, the air screw. An air screw isn't an individual device on its own, but a series of innovations that allow lighter-than-air travel. The air screw uses a combination of new light-weight materials, chemically composed gasses, and steam technology.

The Concert of the World

Shortly after the Martian Invasion of 1872, the foreign ministers of the world gathered in Lisbon to discuss the threat from Mars. For a short time, humanity was united in purpose. Agreements were signed and deals brokered for military aid, trade pacts, and scientific exchange. This was known as the Concert of the World.

By 1882, the Martians had not returned, and the world had returned to business as usual. The return to the status quo was most clearly seen in Europe. The Concert of the World was looked upon with disdain and nationalism was all the rage. The race for colonies began in earnest.

The invention of the airship revolutionized transport, commerce, and war. Soon, nations were scrambling to combine these strange new technologies into their own airships. It was clear that the country that could best exploit this new technology would have the advantage. The airship was so revolutionary that everyone was beginning the game anew, on the same playing field.

At the edges of empires, border and colonial flare-ups around the globe increased tension. The Great Powers jockeyed for the resources and material needed to build their airships. Once-stable borders became porous, as airships could simply float over them with little to stop them.

© Brigade Models

The Art of the Possible

By 1914, the world had stabilized. Despite the revolution in technology, the Old Order still held strong. The Great Powers had ridden the waves of nationalism and militarism. They were held together by a loose collection of international laws negotiated by the Tzar of Russia at The Hague in 1904. National airspace was defined, the rights of aerial commerce negotiated, and laws of war written. The breaking of these laws was to be litigated at the Courts of the Hague.

However, the Great Powers quickly used these new rules to nibble at and inflame each other. They could deadlock litigation in the court for months and years, until the crisis was passed, and scapegoats found. Small conflicts would no longer escalate to total war. Brushfire wars and border skirmishes were the new normal.

Basic Principles

Welcome to *Castles in the Sky*.

This game allows you to play out aerial battles between flying battleships fighting in a mythical turn-of-the-century world. The war of the worlds is over, but the World Wars are just beginning. *You* take command of these massive, armored, battleships in the skies around the world! *Your* commands lead your forces to glorious victory or disgraceful defeat. The fate of nations depends on *you*!

You'll find all the rules you need to play *Castles in the Sky* in this book. At first, the number of rules and variables may look daunting. Read the rules first and then play a few games. When you are ready feel free to add more ships, more terrain, and play the more complex scenarios. Don't be afraid to look up rules as you go.

Be warned: the fate of the nation rests in your hands. Good luck and have fun.

What You Need to Play

Here are some guidelines for what you need to play a game of *Castles in the Sky*:

- Models or tokens to represent your airships.
- A flat space to play.
- A measuring device in the Measurement Units you prefer.
- Six-sided dice, preferably 3 groups of 10 in different colors.
- A method to track altitude such as numbered chits, a ten-sided die, or bits of paper.

It is also helpful but not required to have the following additional items:

- A roster of your airships that you can write on.
- Pencil and eraser.
- Chits, tokens, or markers to track various events during the game.
- Space on the table for your notes to track ship details.
- A detailed set of terrain to fly over.

Game Concepts

Before you begin your first game of *Castles in the Sky* there are a few key concepts that you need to understand completely. Understanding these concepts allows you to take full advantage of the game mechanics.

Altitude

The first thing you need to understand is that *Castles in the Sky* is a three-dimensional game on a two-dimensional board. Airships operate at various altitudes; this is indicated by a number range of 0–9.

Altitude 0 is ground level. A ship that descends to altitude 0 must either land or crash. Altitude 1 is large hills, with altitude 2 to 3 being large mountains. Altitude 4 would be for the highest mountains in the world! Most terrestrial terrain is not over altitude 3.

The highest altitude is altitude 9, and ships operating at that height require special breathing and anti-cold weather gear. Few airships can operate at that altitude for long. It is currently impossible for any airship to go above altitude 9, despite the best efforts of brave aeronauts and engineers to try to do so.

It is vital to track an airship's altitude during the game. You can track the altitude of the aircraft a number of ways: you can use a small chit next to the model, a 10-sided die, or a piece of paper on the sideboard. No matter how you track the altitude of an airship, it is considered public information and must be shared with an opponent on request.

Measurements

The game is designed to be model and scale agnostic. There is a wide range of models available for purchase and some people enjoy making their own. However, the rules themselves don't require any particular models.

To help facilitate this, the game uses a generic measurement system. Instead of using traditional measuring, it uses a mechanic called a Measurement Unit (MU). An MU can be any length that a player wishes to fit their play space and models. Therefore, it is up to the players to decide on exactly how long an MU is in their games.

In addition, there are no guidelines or requirements for basing. All measurements use a nominal center point of the model. For most models on flight stands, this is typically where the base connects with the model. However, if a model doesn't have a flight stand use the generalized center of mass on the model. It is best to agree on the center point prior to the start of the game.

By keeping the measurements generic the game can fit any models or space the players wish. I wrote the rules for use with Brigade Models' lovely Imperial Skies range using a Measurement Unit of 1 inch. However, you may wish to use different models and measurements. Feel free to do so!

Rolling Dice

During the game, you will be asked to roll dice to determine an outcome. *Castles in the Sky* uses standard six-sided dice, which we refer to as a d6.

Typically, a roll requires you to roll a number of six-sided dice all at once. This is indicated by a number followed by the abbreviation of "d6". Therefore, if a test asks you to roll three dice, it would be referenced as 3d6. Other times you'll be asked to roll a number of dice equal to one of your ship's statistics, such as "roll your Firepower dice"

You are looking for a Target Number on each d6. A Target Number is the number or above that you need to roll on the die for a success. Typically, this is expressed as the number of d6 to roll with a Target Number (TN) of Number+, like this: "roll Command dice (TN 4+)". In this case you would roll as many six-sided dice as your ship's Command stat, and each die that rolls 4 or higher counts as a success.

Keep track of the number of successes that you roll. The more successes you roll, the more successful the action was.

I find it is helpful to have at least 30 dice in three sets of colors. This allows you to differentiate what dice are for what rolls and roll them all at once. It is also best if you and your fellow players have your own dice, but it is not strictly necessary.

In some case, you will be asked to roll d3. Most people don't have access to a 3-sided die, so roll a normal d6 and use the table below:

D6 Roll	D3 Roll
1–2	1
3–4	2
5–6	3

Friction

In air combat, the skies in the battle space become filled with exploding shells, hot shrapnel, concussive waves, and other debris. Friction represents all the challenges that an airship experiences in combat including small malfunctions, debris on the deck, shellshocked crewmen, broken communication tubes, and lingering smoke clouds; all the small things that make operating an airship at full capacity difficult. This battle friction is represented in the game by friction markers.

A friction marker is placed on the ship when specific criteria are met:

- Every potential hit causes 1 friction.
- Every potential Munition hit causes 1 friction.

- Every Munition destroyed by Point Defense causes 1 friction.
- When a ship collides, rammed, is boarded, or becomes entangled.
- Where the rules say to "place a friction marker".

Friction markers stay with the airship until they can be removed in the End phase. An airship cannot lose a friction marker except in the End phase. If there is more than one friction marker on an airship at a time, record it by stacking them, putting it on the ship's profile, or some similar tracking method.

Friction has the following effects on any ship that has a friction marker:

- No Commands maybe given to a ship with friction.
- The ship's speed is reduced by 1 per friction marker.
- Munitions cannot be launched.
- Damage Control rolls are reduced by 1 die per friction marker.
- Shooting from a ship with one or more friction markers has -1 Firepower for all armaments.

Rules of Thumb

As you play, you may come across odd situations that are not explicitly covered in the rules and other odd edge cases. Use the following rules of thumb when playing:

- If you come up with a fraction, round up.
- If in doubt regarding line of sight, distance, level of obscuring, fire arc, etc. do what is best for the target ship.
- Measurements can be made at any time by any player before committing to an action
- If there is a dispute on the rules always do what is best for the non-active vessel.
- The current condition and stats of a warship are always public information. If an opponent asks for information on a specific vessel you must provide it.

Most Important Rule

The most important rule of *Castles in the Sky* is to have fun. This is a collaborative game where both players are attempting to enjoy themselves and help their opponent have fun too. If you and your opponent are not having fun, the game has failed, and everyone has lost.

Airship Basics

The Great Powers of the world have a variety of airships to call on. Below are the basics of airships.

Airship Category

Typically, airships of the world fall into one of the three categories listed below:

- Escort
- Cruiser
- Battleship

Categories are generally based on the size and role of the airship in the Navy. However, even within these broad categories there is a dizzying variety of designs and classes.

Escorts

Escorts are typically smaller craft that act as the eyes and ears of the fleet. They carry light armaments and thin armor. However, they typically make up for it with speed and maneuverability. Typically, such vessels are only a threat to their larger cousins when in packs.

Escorts may be called frigates, destroyers, cutters, corvettes, patrol boats, torpedo boats, gunboats, and other names.

Cruisers

The cruiser is the workhorse of the new navies. A cruiser is a big, imposing vessel that is well armed and well protected. It is a capital ship and escorts are no match for a cruiser in a straight engagement. They often are the first response of any nation to a threat. Cruisers are good for long range patrolling, commerce raiding, blockading, and "showing the flag" wherever armed might is needed. The core of any Great Power's fleet is the cruiser.

Battleships

The battleship is the largest type of airship. They have the heaviest armor, the biggest guns, the best engines, and are typically the crown jewels of any modern fleet. Battleships have one job: destroy enemy vessels. They are truly castles in the sky and are the hallmark of a Great Power.

Ship Profiles

Every airship has a profile, a set of statistics and numbers that are used in game to determine a vessel's performance. It is made up of the following information:

Ship Name:		Captain:		
Class: Indefatigable	Category: Cruiser	Armor: 7	Operational Cost: 5	
Speed: 2–8	Altitude: 8	Turns: 1/45	Lift: 1	
Armament	**Firepower**	**Power**	**Fire Arc**	**Ammo**
Heavy Battery	–/5/3/1	–/+3/+2/+1	Bow/Port/ Starboard	4+
Heavy Battery	–/5/3/1	–/+3/+2/+1	Stern/Port/Starboard	4+
Light Battery	–/3/1/–	–/+1/–/–	Bow/Port/Starboard	5+
Point Defense	2/–/–/–	–/–/–/–	All	–
Air Torpedo	4 (Speed 19)	+2	Bow	–

Ship Name

Every ship is a unique vessel with its own history and background. Larger capital ships are individually named with each nation using their own naming conventions. Escorts are typically designated with a letter and number but may have a ship name as well.

For example, a German battleship might be called *Kaiser Wilhelm*. A German destroyer could be numbered the S-482 and named *Harpoon*.

Captain

This is the name of the Captain. His name is followed by a ranking between 1 and 6. The number is the total Command dice used for Command tests.

Class

Vessels in the same class are very similar in armor and armament. Classes are normally named after the first ship of that class.

Category

The category is the type of vessel. This could be escort, cruiser, or battleship. This dictates some of the key statistics of the vessel. Each nation may have a different designation in the class name, but the category is used for game purposes. For example, the Indefatigable Battlecruiser is Category: Cruiser.

Armor

Armor plate is primarily what protects a ship from enemy fire, but there can be other design features that helps a ship be more resistant to damage as well. This is the strength of the armor to defend from incoming attacks.

Operational Cost

This is the cost to operate the ship. Typically, an engagement has a set amount of Operational Value that is composed of all the Operational Costs of the ships in the fleet. In theory, two ships with a similar operational cost should be an even match in combat.

Speed

This is how fast a ship can move. The number here is a range of speeds, from the minimum speed to maximum speed. The number listed is how far in MU the vessel moves on the tabletop in one activation. There are certain commands and situations that allow a ship to go slower or faster.

Altitude

There are three dimensions in air combat. The airship can move between altitude bands as needed to maneuver. This number represents the highest altitude band the ship can safely reach in the battlespace. Some ships can fly higher than others.

Turns

This indicates how sharply a vessel can turn. Ships can only turn a set number of degrees a certain number of times during their movement. This is expressed as the number of turns, with the degrees allowed per turn after the slash.

Lift

The Lift rating measures the power of the air screw. It determines how fast a ship can ascend or descend, and accelerate or decelerate.

Armaments

This section describes the stats used for a ship's armaments.

In the Post-Martian World, there are a number of different weapon systems from various sized cannons, machine guns, and quick-firing deck guns, to air torpedoes and air mines. However, despite the vast array of weaponry, they all use the following statistics to determine their performance.

Range Bands

There are 4 range bands and typically a ship's guns have different firepower ratings in each band. They are:

- Point Blank: Contact with the ship
- Close Range: Up to 8MU
- Mid Range: Up to 16MU
- Long Range: Up to 24MU

A battery's range bands are separated by slashes such as the following:

Point Blank/Close range/Mid range/Long range

For example, a ship's battery may read -/5/3/1. If there is a dash in a range band, the gun can not fire at that range. At Close range it uses 5 dice, Mid range 3 dice, and 1 die at long range.

Munitions and other special attacks have one firepower no matter the range. This is discussed in more detail later.

Armament	Firepower	Power	Fire Arc	Ammo
Heavy Battery	–/5/3/1	–/+3/+2/+1	Bow/Port/ Starboard	4+
Heavy Battery	–/5/3/1	–/+3/+2/+1	Stern/Port/Starboard	4+
Light Battery	–/3/1/–	–/+1/–/–	Bow/Port/Starboard	5+
Point Defense	2/–/–/–	–/–/–/–	All	–
Air Torpedo	4 (Speed 19)	+2	Bow	–

An example of a ship's armament.

Firepower

Firepower is measured by a single number and is the number of dice you roll when firing the weapon. Various modifiers affect the number of dice you need to roll, such as Speed, target, Commands, range, etc. These are discussed in more detail later (see page 22).

Each armament usually has a different Firepower for each range band.

Power

A bigger gun usually has a greater chance to penetrate an opposing airship's hull. The higher the number the better. A weapon usually has a different Power depending on the range band. Shorter ranges usually grant greater Power.

Fire Arc

The space around a naval vessel is divided into four fire arcs. An arc is a field of fire for a weapon system. These facings are bow, port, starboard, and stern. See page 21 for a diagram showing the arcs.

The ship's profile tells you into which arc a weapon system can fire. It is common for a weapon system to be capable of firing in more than one arc, thanks to technology like turrets. However, it may only fire in one arc per shooting phase. The only exception to this is Point Defense weapons, which are discussed in further detail later in these rules (see page 24).

All measurements (moving, shooting, etc.) are made from the center point of the ship, where the four fire arcs cross. Typically, it corresponds to where the flying stand connects with the model or the center of mass of the model.

Ammo

Airships can't carry an unlimited number of shells and there are a number of reasons a ship's guns could be temporarily out of action, such as loader malfunctions, breech jams, lack of ammo in the turret, or damage.

The number here is the Target Number when an airship is called upon to make an Ammo test.

The Rules of Engagement

Game Turn

Everything is madness and chaos in an air battle. Of course, that is no way to play a game. Therefore, in an attempt to regulate all of this madness, we use a turn-based activation system.

A turn-based activation system breaks the game down into the key elements of game play, then proceeds through each of those elements one at a time. Each game element is called a phase. During each phase, the two sides trade off activating their forces for the phase they are playing. This is known as alternate activation.

A turn ends when all phases are complete. A game ends when the scenario's victory conditions have been met or after a pre-determined number of turns has elapsed.

The game turn is designed to keep both players engaged in the game as much as possible at all times. You'll constantly interact with your opponent.

The game turn is composed of the following phases:

- Initiative phase
- Movement phase
- Battle phase
- End phase

Initiative Phase

This phase determines who has the first activation in each phase of this game turn. In addition, each player generates a dice pool to issue commands to their fleet. This is the shortest phase, as it is generally a single dice roll.

Movement Phase

Players take turns moving their airships through the sky. All maneuvering, collisions, ramming, and boarding attempts take place in this phase.

Battle Phase

Both players take turns resolving their shooting and launching Munitions. This phase ends when all eligible airships have had an opportunity to fire.

End Phase

This is the wrap-up phase. Players determine damage, clean up the board, update their ship profiles, and prepare for the next turn. Damage is applied, special events occur, repairs are made, friction is resolved, and more.

Initiative Phase

The Initiative phase is the shortest phase of the game turn, consisting of a single dice roll. However, it dictates the flow of later phases. In addition, it generates a pool of Commands that can be used during the game turn to augment the abilities of various airships. There is more on this in the Commands section (see page 31).

Roll for Initiative

Both players determine the Command dice of their force commander. Each side has a command ship, which is where the fleet commander hangs his flag. The command ship's Command dice are used for the Initiative roll. The command ship is always the ship with the highest Armor value at the start of the game. If two ships have the same Armor, you may pick which is the command ship.

Note that the command ship isn't always the ship with the most Command dice. Since Command dice are randomly determined for each ship it is possible for the command ship to have the fewest Command dice.

The two opposing players roll their command ships' Command dice (TN 4+). The player with the most successes is the winner. In the case of a tie, the commander with the highest number of Command dice wins. If both players have the same number of Command dice, roll again until a winner is determined.

The player who wins the Initiative roll chooses whether to activate their fleet first or second. Once they choose first or second activation, it applies to each phase in the game turn.

Augmenting Command Dice for Initiative

Escorts act as the eyes and ears of the fleet. They are designed for reconnaissance, scouting, and spying. This allows them to funnel intelligence to the commander to evaluate and act on.

During the Initiative phase each active escort ship in the fleet, up to a maximum of 6, gives the commander an additional Command die for Initiative. This represents their scouting, signaling, and patrol functions.

Losing the Command Ship

If a command ship is ever crippled, sunk, or strikes its colors it can no longer function as the command ship. The commander is too busy saving the ship and themselves. Thankfully, air navies have a robust command hierarchy that gives command to another officer in the fleet.

Leadership is shifted to the captain of the airship with next highest starting Armor value. If more than one ship qualifies, the player chooses which is the new command ship. It is likely that this will change the number of Command dice used for the Initiative roll.

Generating the Command Pool

Every success rolled on the Command dice during the Initiative roll is set aside in a Command pool and tracked for the turn. These successes allow the commander the ability to issue Commands to a ship. A commander cannot issue more Commands than they have in their Command pool. The Command pool is created fresh each Initiative phase; unused Commands are lost.

The number of successes that were generated by the Initiative Roll for the Command Pool is public knowledge and must be revealed if asked.

Initiative Phase Ends

The Initiative phase ends once Command Pools are created, and the winning player has chosen to go first or second in all following phases.

Movement Phase

Aerial naval combat is not static. It is dynamic and ever-changing. In the Movement Phase your fleet maneuvers against your foes. The commander who masters the art of maneuver is on the path to victory.

The player who is going first chooses a ship to activate. A ship can only be activated once per Movement Phase.

When the activated ship has completed its Movement Phase, including determining the results of boarding, ramming, collision, etc., the other player then chooses a ship to activate. Players take turns alternating activation until all ships have been activated and moved. All ships must activate during the Phase, even if they can't move.

If a fleet has more ships to move than their opponent, they simply activate and complete the move of any remaining ships until all ships have been activated.

The Movement Sequence

Speed, Altitude, Turns, and Lift are all important during the Movement Phase.

Class: Minotaur	Category: Cruiser	Armor: 8	Operational Cost: 7
Speed: 2–7	Altitude: 8	Turns: 2/45	Lift: 1

When a player nominates a ship to activate in the Movement phase they use the following sequence:

- Determine Speed: The airship can use its air screw to change speed. The vessel can increase or decrease its speed by a number equal to or less than its Lift rating. It can't go above its maximum speed rating or below its minimum speed rating.
- Move: The vessel moves in a straight line forward its current speed in MU.
- Turn: The vessel can initiate a turn at any point during the move. A turn is changing the direction of the ship a number of degrees to port (left) or starboard (right). A vessel can perform one turn for each point in its Turn profile, up to the degrees listed.

- Change Altitude: The ship can choose to change its altitude once at any time during its movement. The airship can rise one altitude band per rating in its Lift stat, losing 1MU of speed per altitude band gained. It can't go higher than its Altitude stat. It may dive one altitude band per Lift rating, gaining 1MU of speed per drop in altitude.
- Complete Move: Resolve any boarding, ramming or collisions. Record any changes in speed and altitude.

Determine Speed

This is the first step of the Movement process. The decision to add, reduce, or maintain current speed is made before any other movement occurs.

A ship may increase or decrease speed up to its Lift rating. A ship can't go faster than its maximum speed or slower than its minimum speed without stalling.

Each point of speed is equal to 1MU of movement.

Move

The ship must move the number of MU indicated by its current speed. The player may choose to initiate a turn and/or altitude change at any point during the move.

Turn

To make a turn follow this process:

- Declare you are making a turn.
- Move the airship at least 2MU forward.
- Pivot your airship in place up to the degrees available in the ship's profile.
- Move the airship forward another 2MU.

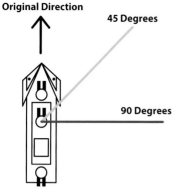

Original Direction

45 Degrees

90 Degrees

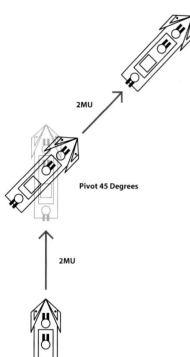

2MU

Pivot 45 Degrees

2MU

The airship can choose to turn at any point while it is moving. However, it doesn't simply pivot in place. The vessel has momentum that must be accounted for. To represent this, a ship must make a forward movement of at least 2MU before executing the turn. If for some reason the ship can't do so, then it can't initiate the turn.

Then pivot the model up to the number of degrees to port or starboard allowed on its profile.

After the pivot is completed, the ship must move at least 2MU forward. If it can't move the 2MU, the turn cannot be executed.

After the second mandatory move is completed, the turn is finished. The vessel may continue its movement phase normally. However, the 4MU used to conduct the turn count against the total move.

A vessel can execute one turn per point of Turn in its profile. The ship can use all its turns at once, or at different points during the Move. However, a ship cannot make more turns than is allowed in its profile.

Altitude Change

A ship may change altitude bands up or down equal to its Lift once per turn. A vessel doesn't have to use its full Lift characteristic.

Changing altitude changes the ship's speed as well. If an airship loses altitude, it gains 1 speed per altitude band. If it gains altitude, it loses 1 speed per altitude band. The new speed takes immediate effect and may impact any remaining move that the ship can perform.

Complete Move

After all turns and lifts have been completed move the ship in a straight line until all remaining speed has been used.

Stalling

A ship can't go faster or slower than its Speed characteristic allows or above/below its Altitude range without stalling. The ship completes its move using its current speed, then stalls.

When a ship stalls, the player can't change speed or altitude, or turn the vessel until the stall has been resolved and the engine restarted.

If a ship is stalled during the End phase, it slows 1 speed per its Lift rating and loses 1 altitude.

Recovering from a Stall

When activated in subsequent Movement phases, the ship can attempt to restart its engine by making a Command test.

- If the ship is still above maximum Speed the ship stays stalled.
- If the ship is at or below maximum Speed the stall can be recovered.
- If the ship is below minimum Speed the stall can be recovered.
- If the ship is above maximum Altitude the ship stays stalled.
- If the ship is at or below maximum Altitude the stall can be recovered.

Roll the ship's Command dice (TN 4+). If at least one success is rolled the engine is restarted and the ship can be activated as normal in subsequent turns. Re-starting the Engine is the airship's Movement Activation this turn.

Collisions

The sky is a big place, so a collision seems unlikely. However, airships are big and slow to change course. When they are operating in tight formations and among enemy vessels, accidents can and do happen. Many careers have been ruined by a poorly timed turn that resulted in a collision.

Determine the results of a collision immediately when it occurs. A collision occurs whenever two vessels at the same altitude would come in contact with each other during the Movement Phase.

A collision is not an intentional act, but an accident of maneuver.

Collision Damage

Each ship takes 1d3 hits. Add +1 Power per hit for each category difference when a larger ship collides with a smaller ship (Battleship being the largest, then Cruiser, and finally Escort being the smallest).

A collision causes 1 Friction per hit. Both ships become entangled.

Hits from a collision can be reduced by Armor or Commands as normal. Damage from a collision is resolved as normal in the End phase (see page 27).

Ramming

Unlike a collision, a ram is an intentional attempt to crash one ship into another. Most sane captains don't attempt to ram as the potential to damage your own vessel is too great. However, desperate times call for desperate measures.

When activating a ship with the intent to ram an opponent, the player must declare the ram and the target.

The ramming airship maneuvers to come into contact with the target airship at the same altitude band.

If the airship fails to make contact, complete the movement as normal. However, the ramming ship receives 1 friction.

If the airship connects, then both ships make a Command test (TN 4+).

- If the ramming ship has scored more successes, they have successfully rammed. Every success more than the enemy ship's is considered a hit.
- If the defender wins, the ramming ship receives a hit for every success more than the attacker's result.

Add +1 Power to each hit per size category difference (Battleship being the largest, then Cruiser, and finally Escort being the smallest).

Ramming hits can be reduced be Armor or Commands as normal. Damage from a ram is resolved as normal in the End phase.

A ram causes 1 friction on both ships, and an additional friction per hit.

The ships become Entangled.

Entangling

Airships may become entangled with each other when they collide or ram each other. Essentially, the damage to their structures locks them in a dangerous embrace. When two ships are entangled, neither can move. Instead, they are subject to the rules for being stalled.

Effects of Being Entangled

The following rules apply to ships that are entangled:

- Movement Phase: Entangled ships can't move, turn, or change altitude. They are stalled, and can't attempt to recover. Entangled airships can attempt to either disentangle or board the enemy.
- Battle Phase: Airships that are Entangled can be targeted by ranged weapons. However, any hits and friction apply to both ships equally. An entangled ship may fire as normal, but all targets count as obscured.
- End Phase: Ships still entangled In the End phase are considered stalled.

Disentangle

To become disentangled, the active ship makes a Command test (TN 4+).

If no successes are rolled, the ship remains entangled and stalled. If a success is rolled, the ship has become disentangled and both ships receive a friction marker.

Once disentangled, the airship can move past the other vessel without causing a further collision. Continue the activation as normal.

Boarding Action

There is no better time to launch a boarding action than when two ships are locked together and entangled. In a boarding action the crews from both ships try to fight their way over to the opponent's airship and cause damage and havoc. The fighting is up close and personal.

A boarding action can only occur when both ships are touching due to a collision, ram, or being entangled.

Boarding actions take place after the results of any collision or ram have been determined.

Vessels that have been reduced to 0 Armor cannot participate in a boarding action.

When a player activates a ship that is in contact with an enemy airship in the Movement Phase the active vessel can initiate a boarding action. Both ships make a Command test (TN 4+).

The ship that scores the most successes has won the boarding action and damages the enemy ship. Every success over the opponent's number of successes reduces the loser's Command dice by 1. If an airship's Command dice reaches 0, additional boarding damage causes hits, which are resolved as normal.

Both ships receive a point of friction.

Landing

When an airship is activated in the Movement Phase, the player can declare that it is landing.

To land, the airship must reduce speed to its slowest possible speed and reduce its altitude to the terrain it is over by the end of the Movement phase.

If completed successfully the airship has landed. A landed airship is treated as a normal ground target for purposes of being attacked.

A landed airship can't participate in the Movement phase. It must be activated, but may only perform a Take-off or take no further action. However, a landed airship can participate in the Battle and End phases as normal.

Take Off

Any airship on the ground can be activated in the Movement phase. Once activated, the ship can choose to take off. To take off the ship moves straight on its current heading at its minimum speed. The airship ends its turn at minimum Altitude and Speed.

It is no longer treated as a ground target and can act as normal in subsequent phases.

Hovering

There are some situations where a ship can reach a minimum speed of 0. In such a case, they can hover in place with no forward momentum.

An airship can choose to pivot while hovering. This operates like a normal turn, but the airship doesn't need the momentum of moving 2MU before and after the turn. Instead, the airship pivots in place up to the Turn rating in its ship profile.

Battle Phase

The Battle Phase is where all the cunning maneuvers of the Movement phase come to a head. It is filled with the roar of cannons, the buzz of air torpedoes, and the devastating blasts of detonating munitions. During this phase opposing fleets fire their guns, launch munitions, and cause damage to their enemies.

Once all ships have completed their Movement Phase, the Battle Phase begins, and no more movement can be executed. Be sure all airships have activated during the Movement Phase before beginning this phase of the game.

In the Battle Phase you attack enemy airships with your weapons. The player with initiative chooses a ship to activate. They determine the results of shooting and munitions. A ship can only be activated once per Battle Phase.

When the activated ship has completed their Battle Phase, the non-active player chooses the next ship to activate. Players take turns alternating activation with their ships until all ships have been activated. All ships must activate during the phase, even if they can't attack.

If a fleet has more ships to activate than their opponent, they simply activate and complete the attacks of any remaining ships until all ships have been activated.

An active ship can choose to resolve its attacks in any order it wishes. However, all weapons firing at the same target should be resolved at the same time. In this case, it is helpful to have different colored dice to differentiate weapon battery attacks, such as red for heavy batteries, yellow for medium batteries, and blue for light batteries. Munitions should be resolved separately from weapon battery attacks.

All weapon batteries use all their Firepower dice on the same target and can't be split, but different batteries can fire at different targets. With the exception of Point Defenses, weapon batteries and munitions only fire once a turn.

Types of Weapon

The Great Powers of the world have devised a myriad of weapons. Each country has their own arsenals and weapons manufacturers. However, weapon systems can be broken down into a few main types:

Direct Fire Weapons: These are typically rifled, breech-loading cannons firing explosive shells at the target in a relatively straight line of fire. Their main target is other airships.

Point Defenses: In addition to the big gun batteries used to attack other airships, a warship has an assortment of smaller caliber machine guns and cannons. These Point Defense weapons are used to defend the vessel from air torpedoes, aeroplanes, sky mines, and more.

Air Torpedoes: The air torpedo was developed shortly after the air screw was discovered. They are ingenious, small, self-propelled warheads that can rise and fall in altitude based on how the propulsion screws and navigation fins are set. This gives them a great versatility in air combat. However, they leave a distinctive smoke trail that leaves them vulnerable to Point Defense fire, unlike a direct-fire explosive shell, and they are slower than their direct-fire brethren. Air torpedoes require special launchers to fire effectively.

Sky Mines: Sky mines are a passive deterrence system designed to interdict the free movement of airships. They are suspended in the air by a variety of mechanisms unique to each Great Power. They loiter in a section of sky, waiting for a passing airship to trigger their

explosive payload. They can only be deployed from ships equipped with special launching devices. Thankfully, sky mines aren't hard to detect by skilled observers.

Aeroplanes: Airships are not the only technological innovation made possible by the air screw. Small one- or two-man aeroplanes have also become popular. These machines have greater speed and maneuverability than the much larger airships, but their small frame limits their firepower. There are two main types of aeroplanes in use in the air fleets: fighters and bombers.

Bombs: Once airships were invented, it didn't take long for the military to start dropping things from them. The first bombs were simply rocks. From these humble beginnings the dreaded aerial bomb came into existence. For the most part the bombs themselves are very simple explosive devices that use gravity to deliver explosive loads to their targets. Bombs can only be dropped from special equipment installed into an airship.

Direct Fire

Direct Fire is the most common type of shooting between warships. Essentially, each ship aims its guns at a target and opens fire. The gunners try to correct misses based on where the previous shells detonated. Direct Fire weapon shells move too fast and are too small to counter with Point Defense weapons.

Follow this sequence:

- Declare Fire
- Determine Target Priority
- Determine Fire Arcs
- Determine Range
- Determine line of sight
- Determine Firepower Dice
- Roll to Hit
- Determine hits
- Make Ammo test

Declare Fire

The Player declares which weapon batteries are firing at which targets. Once the shots are declared, proceed with resolving the attacks.

If a target is determined to be ineligible to be fired upon during the following sequence, the shots automatically miss and the battery must make an Ammo test.

Target Priority

A ship should fire at the closest enemy ship. Many warships have more than one weapon system, so it is possible for the closest target to be different for weapon systems in different arcs. Make target priority checks by individual battery.

A battery can choose to fire at any target they want, however, if they wish to fire at an enemy ship other than the closest, then they must pass a Command test (TN 4+). If a single success is rolled, the battery may choose to fire at any target it wishes. If no successes are rolled, the gunners are too busy adjusting the guns to fire and that battery may not fire at all this turn.

Fire Arcs

As discussed earlier, all ships are divided into four firing arcs. The description of the weapon system tells you into which arc the weapon can fire. Many weapons can fire into more than one arc. Point Defense weapons, which are discussed in further detail later, don't have firing arcs.

If no targets fall within a weapon's fire arc, then the weapon can't be fired.

It is possible that an enemy airship can be in more than one fire arc at a time. This means weapons that can fire in either arc may fire at that ship. This allows a clever commander to stack additional firepower on an enemy airship.

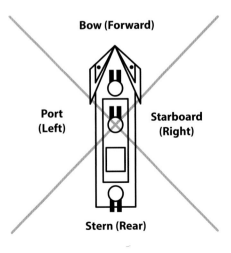

Range

Most of the airships of the Great Powers use roughly the same type of breech-loading cannon with explosive shells. As such, they all have the same basic capabilities, despite being manufactured across Europe.

As mentioned in the ship profiles, the basic ranges are:

- Point Blank: In contact with the ship
- Close Range: Up to 8MU
- Mid-Range: Up to 16MU
- Long Range: Up to 24MU

To determine the range of a shot, simply draw a straight line between the mid-point of the firing ship and the mid-point of the target ship. The length of this line is the range.

If the line is longer than the range of the weapon, the shots automatically miss. The guns are still considered to have fired, but they simply fail to hit the target by default. Make an Ammo test for the battery.

Line of Sight

Line of sight is required to effectively fire Direct Fire weapons. Typically, when you measure for range, you also determine line of sight. If a line of sight can't be established, the shot can't be made with that weapon battery.

Some terrain impacts line of sight differently, so consult the terrain section of the rules for complete details of what does and does not block line of sight. Altitude changes do not impact range or line of sight and you can fire at ships at different altitudes.

Determine Firepower Dice

All Direct Fire weapons use TN 4+ to determine hits.

Each point of Firepower in a weapon's profile allows you to roll one die. So, if a weapon battery has Firepower 4, you roll 4 dice.

There are situations that modify the number of Firepower dice you can roll when attacking. These are called modifiers, and add to or subtract from the number of dice rolled. Modifiers stack, so it is possible for more than one modifier to apply. If the modifiers reduce the Firepower dice to 0 or below, the shots automatically miss; make an Ammo test.

Firepower Modifier	Firepower Dice
Each altitude band the target is above or below the firing ship	-1
Each level of category difference between weapon and target	-1
Firing ship has a friction marker	-1
Target is moving at speed 10+	-1
Target obscured by smoke, terrain, or other airships	-1

Weapon Battery Category vs. Target Size

Different caliber weapons are designed to hit different sized targets. For example, a battleship's heavy batteries are intended to target other battleships. They are ill-suited for attacking smaller craft such as cruisers and escorts. For such targets, they are often fitted with smaller caliber guns.

Weapon Battery	Intended Target
Heavy Battery	Battleship
Medium Battery	Cruiser
Light Battery	Escort

When a weapon fires on a target that is inappropriate for its type, the Firepower of the weapon is reduced 1 die per difference between the battery size and the target category.

For example, if a German cruiser fires its medium battery at a Japanese destroyer, the modifier would by -1 Firepower. However, if the same German cruiser then fires its light battery at the Japanese destroyer there would be no Firepower reduction as the battery size and the ship category match.

Roll to Hit

Roll the Firepower dice (TN 4+) based on the ship's profile, range, and Firepower modifiers. Count up the successes.

Damage

Airships are equipped with strong armor plates and reinforced hulls. They are tough to damage, even with the most advanced artillery and high explosives. To counter these defenses, each weapon has a Power rating.

For every potential hit roll a die and add the Power rating of the weapon. Compare the result to the ship's Armor rating. If the result is the same as the Armor rating of the ship or higher, the shot has inflicted 1 damage. If it is less, no damage has occurred and the shell just rings off the armor plates.

For every Power roll to be made, place 1 friction marker on the target ship. Every successful hit that equals or beats the target's Armor rating will cause damage. Save the number of damaging hits to resolve in the End phase. This can be tracked on the ship's profile, markers, or any manner you wish.

Ammo Test

Airships can't carry unlimited ammunition and occasionally suffer technical malfunctions when firing repeatedly. When a ship fires and fails to roll any hits, it must make an Ammo test. An Ammo test is also required if the target is determined to be ineligible after shooting attacks have been declared.

To make an Ammo test complete the following:

- Roll the ship's Command dice; the target number is in the weapon profile.
- If a success is rolled, the weapon is still operational.
- If no successes are rolled, the weapon may not fire again until fixed.

There are two ways to try to bring the weapon systems back online:

- Successfully issue a Reload command to the airship.
- Pass a Repair test in the End Phase.

A failed Ammo test represents weapon jams, problems in the loading process, electrical malfunctions, or getting more shells brought up from the magazine.

Point Defense Weapons

Warships are ringed by a variety of small caliber weapons to help protect it from enemy attacks such as air torpedoes, sky mines, and aeroplanes. When these types of attacks contact a vessel the Point Defenses are triggered to defend against the attack.

Use the following process:

- Point Defense results are determined before munitions and aeroplane attacks.
- Roll the Firepower of the Point Defense (TN 4+).
- For every success rolled, reduce the Firepower of the incoming attack by 1.
- For each success rolled the airship gains a friction marker.

Escort Point Defense Screen

Escorts are intended to use their Point Defense weapons to help screen larger airships. If an escort is within 2MU and 1 altitude of another airship, they can augment the Point Defenses of their fellow airship. The Firepower of the two Point Defenses is combined.

For example, a Japanese Sakura-class destroyer is within 2MU and 1 altitude of a Tsushima-class cruiser. A Russian airship fires air torpedoes at the cruiser. The Tsushima class normally has a Point Defense of 2. However, the Sakura can add her 2 Firepower of Point Defense to the Tsushima. That gives the Tsushima 4 Firepower dice against the incoming air torpedoes.

Air Torpedoes

When a ship fires its air torpedoes, it uses specially fitted launch tubes to guide the torpedo at the target. Prior to launch, gunners can set the air torpedo to gain or lose altitude, giving the air torpedo a larger, more reliable firing solution than direct-fire cannons. This has made them a popular weapon. However, setting up and firing an air torpedo properly takes additional time and expertise.

Air torpedoes fire like a normal Direct Fire weapon, with the following exceptions:

- Air torpedoes are fired in batches, with each point of Firepower representing 1 torpedo that attacks separately.
- Air torpedoes fly in a straight line up to their speed rating.
- Air torpedoes can target an airship up or down up to 3 altitude bands from the firing ship.
- Point Defense weapons always fire before determining the results of an air torpedo attack.
- The torpedo attacks when it contacts a vessel.
- Air torpedoes never suffer from modifiers when attacking.

Roll the Firepower dice of the torpedoes (TN 4+).

If a failure is rolled, that torpedo continues on to the next potential target. If it goes its full distance without finding a target, it runs out of power and falls away harmlessly.

A success generates a potential hit on the target. For every hit a Power roll must made to determine if it causes damage. Place 1 friction marker on the target ship. The Firepower of the air torpedo is reduced 1 for every hit inflicted on the initial target. Every successful hit that equals or beats the target's Armor rating will cause damage. Save the number of damaging hits to resolve in the End phase. This can be tracked on the ship's profile, markers, or any manner you wish. The rest of the Air Torpedoes continue in a straight line at the target altitude, and will continue to potentially hit any other airships they come in contact with, they are reduced to 0 firepower, or they run out of distance.

Air torpedoes must be reloaded using a Command before they can fire again.

Sky Mines

The sky mine is a passive area-denial weapon. They can only be deployed by airships with specialized launchers and equipment. It requires skilled sailors and specialists to properly arm the mines and deploy them without causing an on-board detonation. Sky mines are left behind the airship when deployed.

Sky mines are used as follows:

- Sky mines are always deployed up to their Speed rating in the fire arc of the vessel using them.
- They deploy at the same altitude as the airship when launched.
- Once deployed, they remain stationary.
- The Firepower rating is the number of mine counters deployed; each requires a counter about 1" or 25mm in diameter.
- Point Defense weapons always fire before determining the results of a sky mine attack
- Sky mines attack if they touch a vessel within 1 altitude band difference.
- Sky mines never suffer from modifiers when attacking

Roll 1d6 (TN 4+) for each base that a vessel comes in contact with. On a failure it fails to detonate, but the mine counter is removed and a Friction Marker is placed on the airship. On a success it is a potential hit. For every success a Power roll will be made. A Successful Power roll causes 1 damage.

All Damage is resolved in the End phase.

© Brigade Models

Once deployed, the launchers are empty and more sky mines can be deployed only after a successful Reload command.

Sky Mine Sweepers

Any airship that is equipped with sky mines has the equipment to act as a mine sweeper. They can safely remove one mine marker per Firepower of their own mines each turn.

Mine sweepers don't gain a friction marker when removing mines.

If the mine sweeper comes in contact with more sky mines then they can safely remove, any additional mines attack as normal.

Aeroplanes

Aeroplanes can only launch from ships that have special launching platforms and decks. Specialty crews are needed to service, maintain, and fly aeroplanes. However, they offer a wider variety of maneuver than any other weapon system.

Aeroplanes are used as follows:

- Aeroplanes launch in the Battle phase in a straight line up to their full speed rating at the altitude band of the launching ship. They are deployed from the fire arc of the launcher.
- Ships may launch one aeroplane marker per rating of Firepower. All markers start touching each other. When launched, the farthest aeroplane may not exceed their speed rating. Each aeroplane marker must be designated as a Fighter or Bomber as it is deployed, and each aeroplane type should have a distinctive marker. Aeroplane markers are generally 25–30mm in diameter.
- Aeroplanes can turn and move freely, but can't move further than their speed rating. They can change one altitude band with no change to speed. All touching aeroplane markers must be moved as a group. Aeroplanes move in both the Battle and End phases.
- Aeroplanes attack as soon as they come in contact with a potential target. Each aeroplane marker has a single point of Firepower.
- No airship can have more aeroplanes deployed at one time than the Firepower rating of their launcher. Once deployed, aeroplanes can only be launched again after a successful reload command.

Fighters

Fighters primarily attack other aircraft.

They remove other aeroplanes on a one-for-one basis when they come into contact. Both markers are removed; they are assumed to be destroyed, or scatter back to their home base to refuel and rearm.

Each fighter aeroplane token that comes in contact with an airship reduces the target airship's Point Defense Firepower by 1. This occurs **before** Point Defense can fire. The aeroplane is removed from play, assumed to be destroyed or to return to rearm and refuel. An airship attacked by aeroplanes gains a friction marker.

Bombers

Bombers attack their target with rockets, short range air torpedoes, small cannons, and small bombs.

Point Defense weapons always fire before determining the results of a bomber attack.

Bomber aeroplanes attack when they come in contact with an enemy vessel. The number of bombers in contact is the Firepower of the attack. Bombers never suffer from modifiers when attacking

Roll 1d6 (TN 4+) for each bomber that comes into contact with an enemy vessel; on a success it is a potential hit. For every hit a Power roll must made to determine if it causes damage. Place 1 friction marker on the target ship

All Damage is resolved in the End phase.

After attacking, the bomber marker is removed from play. They are assumed to scatter and return to their airship to refuel and rearm.

Place a friction marker on an airship hit by a bomber.

Bombs

Like air torpedoes and sky mines, bombs require special delivery methods. Unlike most weapon systems, they are relatively simple devices. The hard part is getting them to hit their targets. Bombs are typically used on ground targets, but can theoretically be dropped on any target lower than the bombing airship.

Bombs fire like a normal Direct Fire weapon, with the following exceptions:

- Point Defense weapons always fire before determining the results of a bomb attack.
- Bombs are deployed up to their speed rating straight from the fire arc of the launcher, typically the rear.
- Bombs are considered to immediately drop to the target's altitude.
- Bombs attack when they touch a target.
- Bombs lose 1 Firepower rating per altitude band they drop towards a target

Roll 1d6 (TN 4+) for each point of bomb Firepower. A success is a hit on the target. For every success a Power roll must be made to determine if it causes damage. Place a friction marker on any airship that is successfully bombed.

On a failure, the bomb is assumed to scatter off target and does no damage.

All Damage is resolved in the End phase.

Bombs must be reloaded using a Command before they can be fired again.

Ground Combat

Airships may dominate the skies, but ground forces are still needed to hold territory. Competition between the Great Powers is primarily concerned with territorial gains. Therefore, the ground-pounders always play a role in modern warfare. However, air power is often called on to eliminate or remove ground forces such as dug-in troops, fortresses, or other targets.

Bombing Ground Targets

Ground targets come in all different types. They can be troop formations, trains, buildings, or fortifications. For game purposes they are considered immobile and at the altitude band of the ground or the height of any terrain they are placed on. They cannot use Commands.

Before the game begins, ground targets should be assigned an Armor rating between 1 and 10. The harder the target, the higher the rating. A ground target is destroyed if its Armor reaches 0.

Ground targets use the following damage table using a 2d6:

Bombing Ground Target Table	
Roll	Damage
2	No Damage
3–10	-1 Armor
11–12	Target destroyed!

Shelling Ground Targets

Airships without bombs may attempt to shell a target using their guns. They must be within range of the target. Ground targets are shelled using the same method as attacking an airship.

End Phase

After both sides have completed their Movement and Battle Phases, the End Phase begins. The End Phase is the final phase of the turn and completes key activities and sets-up the next turn.

The player with Initiative gets to complete their actions in each portion of the End phase first. When the player with initiative has completed all relevant actions, then play moves to the inactive player.

For example, the active player moves and resolves one aeroplane attack, then the inactive player

does so. Once done with aeroplanes, the active player applies damage to their airships, and when they are done, play moves to the Inactive player. Continue this process until the End phase is completed.

The following action occur in the End phase. They occur in the following order.

1. Move aeroplanes
2. Apply damage
3. Resolve stalls/sinking
4. Strike your colors
5. Repair tests
6. Remove friction

1. Move Aeroplanes

The complete rules for aeroplanes are covered in the Battle Phase section (see page 26). Aeroplanes move in the End Phase, to represent the greater speed of aeroplanes compared to airships. If they come into contact with an Airship, they can attack as normal.

The player with initiative chooses the first aeroplane or group he wishes to move, moves it, and resolves any attacks. Once complete, the opposing player can choose one of his aeroplane groups and does the same. Alternate activating aeroplanes and groups until all aeroplanes have been moved.

2. Apply Damage

The player resolves all hits from the Battle phase and determines the results. Roll once on the Damage Table for each damage to determine the effect. All damage is resolved with the Damage Table.

The Damage Table

For each hit roll 2d6 and add the results together. Consult the table below:

Damage Table	
2d6 Roll	**Damage**
2	Fire! – Critical Damage
3	Bridge Damaged – Critical Damage
4	Weapon Destroyed! – Critical Damage
5	Rudder Jammed! – Critical Damage
6	Screw Fouled! – Critical Damage
7–10	Hull Breach!
11	Ship Crippled!
12	Ship Explodes!

Fire!

A Fire has ignited in the bowels of the ship. It is every air sailor's worst nightmare! Every turn the fire rages requires another roll on the Damage Table. If Fire is rolled again, re-roll until a non-Fire result is reached. Note this result on the ship's profile or add a marker until the fire is repaired.

Bridge Damaged!

A shell has struck close to the bridge and riddled it with shrapnel and debris. The bridge crew is shaken and injured. Reduce the ship's Command dice by 1 and reduce the ship's Armor by 1. If the Command dice are reduced to 0 it is assumed that the Captain was killed. If the Captain has been killed, only apply the Armor damage for subsequent Bridge Damaged results.

Weapon Destroyed!

One of the main turrets or armories was hit! Randomly determine one battery or weapon system. It is unusable until it is repaired. Note the damage on the ship's profile or otherwise track the damage in any mutually agreeable way. Reduce the ship's Armor by 1.

Rudder Jammed!

The delicate maneuvering system used to direct the air screw has been damaged. The ship's turn rating is reduced by 1, to a minimum of 0. If turns are all ready at 0, then just apply the Armor damage. Reduce the ship's Armor by 1.

Screw Fouled!

The air screw has been damaged slowing the ship. The ship's maximum Speed is reduced by 2 for every damaging hit! Normal stalling rules apply for going below minimum Speed. If the airship already has a maximum speed of 0 ignore the special damage and only apply the Armor reduction. Reduce the ship's Armor by 1.

Hull Breach

The ship has taken serious damage to the superstructure and armored belt. Reduce the ship's Armor by 1.

Ship Crippled!

The ship no longer responds as ordered. She is starting to go down! Once a ship is Crippled, it cannot be repaired. It is considered to be sinking. Note this on the ship's profile or suitably mark the airship on the board.

Ship Explodes!

The ship explodes in a spectacular fireball from the ammunition or air screw combusting. Any craft within 1d6MU suffers 1d3 hits at Power +1d3. The model is removed from the board.

Airships at 0 Armor

If an airship's Armor is reduced to 0 due to damage, it starts sinking. In addition, it needs to make a Strike Your Colors test (see page 30). The normal rules for sinking apply. Roll as normal for damage from additional hits.

Sinking

Airships that are Crippled or have their Armor reduced to 0 start to sink. A sinking ship can't fire weapons, ram, or initiate a boarding action.

Once an airship is sinking, it loses speed equal to its Lift rating and drops 1 altitude band in each End phase until the ship reaches Speed 0 and Altitude 0. At Altitude 0, the ship crashes and is removed from play.

Overkill

An airship can have its Armor reduced below 0. When it reaches more than negative half its starting Armor, the airship explodes as per the rules for Ship Explodes! on the Damage Table.

3. Resolve Stalls/Sinking

Airships that are stalled or sinking are moved according to the rules for sinking. Update their speed and altitude accordingly.

4. Strike Your Colors

If a ship has taken too much punishment a captain may lose heart and choose to strike their colors. In this situation, the captain is giving up the fight in an attempt to save their ship.

During the End Phase, players can take alternating turns making Strike Your Colors tests. The player with initiative can choose the first airship to test. A player can also choose to simply have the airship strike its colors without rolling. Once the test is complete, the opposing player then does the same with one of his airships. This continues until all airships that must make a Strike Your Colors test has done so.

When to take a Strike Your Colors Test

An airship needs to take a Strike Your Colors test in the following situations:

- If it is Stalled.
- If it is Sinking.
- If it is Crippled.
- If it is Entangled.
- If it has lost half or more of its starting Armor value.

Making a Strike Your Colors Test

The ship rolls its Command dice (TN 4+) a single success is required to pass a strike your colors test, however it is modified by the following conditions:

- One additional success is needed per Critical Damage on the airship (screw fouled, bridge destroyed, etc.).
- One additional success is needed if the airship is at 0 Armor or less.

If successful, the ship can continue to fight on, but all current damage and effects still remain.

It is possible that a ship could auto-fail this test if the captain doesn't have sufficient Command dice to pass the test.

Failing a Strike Your Colors Test

If the roll fails, the airship has chosen to strike its colors and refrain from further combat. The crew is focused on survival in a critically damaged ship. An airship that has struck their colors can no longer participate in any attacks on other ships or accept Commands.

Instead, such vessels must do one of the following:

- Leave the board as quickly as possible.
- Attempt to Land.
- Nothing, if it is unable to act.

Once a ship fails a strike your colors test, it is "destroyed" for Armor loss considerations at the end of a scenario. There is no additional benefit attacking a ship that has struck their colors.

5. Repair Tests

A ship may receive critical damage during a battle. Critical damage is noted on the Damage Table. Critical damage can be repaired by dedicated engineering crews ready to go into the bowels of the ship to repair vital components and weld together vital plating. Players may attempt to repair critical damage or failed Ammo tests. Destroyed Armor can't be repaired.

Roll Command dice (TN 4+) for the ship. Each success repairs one critical damage or Ammo test of the player's choice.

6. Remove Friction

Roll the Command dice of your command ship plus any bonus Command dice from escorts and add up the results. The number rolled is the number of friction points that must be removed from the board. A player must remove friction up to the number rolled, even if it is on enemy vessels; they can't remove fewer friction markers than rolled. Once the Active player is done removing friction, the inactive player does the same. It is possible for all friction to be removed from play.

Commands

Commands are orders given by a ship's captain to focus the crew on specific tasks outside of their normal duties. Commands need to be done immediately and done right. As a result, normal operations may suffer while Commands are being carried out. Commands are used to improve a ship's ability to perform specific functions varying by the Command given.

When Can You Give a Command

Commands can be issued while the ship is active. This can be in the Move or the Battle Phase, at any point during its Activation.

Each Fleet has a specific number of Commands that can be given in a turn. This is determined by the Initiative roll. Each success when rolling for Initiative allows a single Command to be given. Once all Commands have been given, no additional Commands can be made that turn.

An airship can only be given a single Command during the turn. The crew is too busy obeying that command to be able to respond to any additional Commands.

How to Give a Command

When a command is issued, the ship must make a Command test. Roll the ship's Command dice (TN 4+). On any success, the test is passed. The command is carried out and the ship can take advantage of the command's benefits and suffer its drawbacks.

If no successes are rolled, the Command test fails and the ship doesn't receive the benefits of the command.

List of Commands
Movement Commands

Come About
- **Benefits:** The airship leans heavily into its turn to change course rapidly. The airship can make a single turn up to double its normal turn radius: 45 degree becomes 90 and 90 becomes a 180.
- **Drawbacks:** The airship may not change altitude while performing this maneuver. The airship may only use Direct Fire and Point Defense weapons. All Firepower is reduced by 2.

Crash Dive
- **Benefits:** The ship may double its Lift statistic for the purposes of losing altitude. Normal speed changes apply, as do the rules for stalling.
- **Drawbacks:** The airship may only use Direct Fire and Point Defense weapons. All Firepower is reduced by 2.

Emergency Climb
- **Benefits:** The airship may double its Lift statistic for the purposes of gaining altitude. Normal speed changes apply, as do the rules for stalling.
- **Drawbacks:** The airship may only use Direct Fire and Point Defense weapons. All Firepower is reduced by 2.

Evasive Maneuvers
- **Benefits:** The ship tries to avoid a collision by throwing the wheel hard over. If successful, the collision is avoided. If failed, the collision occurs as normal.
- **Drawbacks:** The airship may only use Direct Fire and Point Defense weapons. All Firepower is reduced by 2.

Full Speed Ahead
- **Benefits:** The Command allows the ship to double its Lift characteristic for the purpose of accelerating.
- **Drawbacks:** While moving so rapidly the ship may only use Direct Fire and Point Defense weapons. All weapon Firepower is reduced by 2. The ship can't execute any turns or altitude changes.

Reverse Engines
- **Benefits:** The ship can double its Lift capabilities for the purpose of decelerating. In addition, a ship can go below its normal speed minimum and even hover without stalling, even if not normally allowed to do so.
- **Drawbacks:** The airship may only use Direct Fire and Point Defense weapons. All Firepower is reduced by 2. The ship can't execute any turns or altitude changes.

Smoke Screen
- **Benefits:** The ship stokes its boilers and generates a cloud of gas, steam, and smoke around itself. Direct fire attacks aimed at this ship are subject to a -1 Firepower modifier, due to the obscuring cloud.
- **Drawbacks:** The airship may only use Direct Fire and Point Defense weapons. All Firepower is reduced by 2.

Battle Commands

Damage Control
- **Benefits:** This command orders more hands to managing damage. The ship can re-roll all failed Repair die.
- **Drawbacks:** The airship may only use Direct Fire and Point Defense weapons. All Firepower is reduced by 2.

Fire for Effect
- **Benefits:** Re-roll missed Direct Fire attacks.
- **Drawbacks:** This command has no effect on Point Defense, air torpedoes, sky mines, bombs, or aeroplanes. These types of weapons may not be fired or deployed when firing for effect. Make Ammo tests for all weapon batteries that fire for effect.

Prepare for Impact!
- **Benefits:** This command gives the ship a special dice roll to resist damage once hits have been determined. For every hit inflicted, roll 1d6 (TN 4+). Every success negates a hit. Remaining hits are converted to damage during the End phase, as normal.
- **Drawbacks:** The airship may only use Direct Fire and Point Defense weapons. All Firepower is reduced by 2.

Reload
- **Benefits:** The ship can fix one inoperable weapon due to a failed Ammo check, or ready air torpedoes, sky mines, bombs, or aeroplanes for use.
- **Drawbacks:** If the test is failed, the weapon system may not be used.

Restart Engines
- **Benefits:** The ship is no longer stalled.
- **Drawbacks:** The airship may only use Direct Fire and Point Defense weapons. All Firepower is reduced by 2.

Air Navies

Here you find the rules needed to field the air navies of the world, including airships from the Great Powers. Each Great Power has their own unique traditions, designs, and line-of-battle.

Using the Line-of-Battle

Each list presents a number of ship types and rules to use in games of *Castles in the Sky*. Each list is divided into the following sections:

Background

This is a brief overview of the force, its structure, and its aims post-Martian invasion. This helps you flesh out the nature and character of your fleet.

Determining Command Dice

Airship commanders are all big personalities with their own foibles and strengths. Some are better than others. Therefore, this section is used to determine the actual Command ability of the ships you select for your fleet. Typically, a ship commander has a rating between 1 and 4 Command dice.

Line-of-Battle

The details for the various ship classes and vessels is found here. These can be combined to create your own air navy fleet to use on the board. You'll find all of the ship types, profiles, and armaments in this section.

British Empire

The British Royal Navy was the first nation to build an airship. From that day forward they were the nation to beat in the new air navy arms race. Since those heady early days the British are no longer the sole masters of the air. It didn't take long for the technology to leak out and other nations to start building ships of their own. However, the British Royal Navy has maintained their lead in the air naval race.

For decades, the British have been focused on maintaining the balance of power on the European continent and with the Great Powers around the world. Their greatest fear is a merger or alliance between nations that would be powerful enough to control Europe and potentially endanger their isles. Therefore, their politics in the Great Power world are focused on dividing allies, aligning with the underdogs, and maintaining the status quo.

In addition to their concerns on the Continent, they also have an extensive colonial empire that spans the globe. The Royal Navy has a number of flying ships deployed across the world to secure His Majesty's interests. This includes bases in the Atlantic Ocean, Pacific Ocean, Africa, Indian Sub-Continent, China, and more. Around the home islands they prefer battleships. Around the world they prefer battlecruisers and cruisers to enforce their will.

Britain's main rivals are Russia, France, and Germany. Their closest allies are the United States and Japan. Other alliances are determined by the needs of the moment.

Command Dice

Determine each captain's Command dice by rolling 1d6 for each ship:

British Empire Command Dice Table	
Roll	**Command dice**
1–2	2
3–4	3
5–6	4

British Line of Battle

Queen Elizabeth Class Battleship				
Class: Queen Elizabeth	Category: Battleship	Armor: 9	Operational Cost: 11	
Speed: 2–6	Altitude: 7	Turns: 1/45	Lift: 1	
Armament	**Firepower**	**Power**	**Fire Arc**	**Ammo**
Heavy Battery	–/6/4/2	–/+5/+3/+2	Bow/Port/ Starboard	4+
Heavy Battery	–/6/4/2	–/+5/+3/+2	Stern/Port/ Starboard	4+
Light Battery	–/3/1/–	–/+1/–/–	Bow/Port/ Starboard	5+
Light Battery	–/3/1/–	–/+1/–/–	Stern/Port/ Starboard	5+
Point Defense	3/–/–/–	–/–/–/–	All	–

Iron Duke Class Battleship				
Class: Iron Duke	Category: Battleship	Armor: 8	Operational Cost: 11	
Speed: 2–6	Altitude: 7	Turns: 1/45	Lift: 1	
Armament	**Firepower**	**Power**	**Fire Arc**	**Ammo**
Heavy Battery	–/7/5/3	–/+3/+2/+1	Bow/Port/ Starboard	4+
Heavy Battery	–/3/2/1	–/+3/+2/+1	Stern/Port/ Starboard	4+
Light Battery	–/4/2/–	–/–/–/–	Bow/Port/ Starboard	5+
Point Defense	2/–/–/–	–/–/–/–	All	–

Indefatigable Class Battlecruiser

Class: Indefatigable	Category: Cruiser	Armor: 7	Operational Cost: 5	
Speed: 2–8	Altitude: 8	Turns: 1/45	Lift: 1	
Armament	**Firepower**	**Power**	**Fire Arc**	**Ammo**
Heavy Battery	–/5/3/1	–/+3/+2/+1	Bow/Port/ Starboard	4+
Heavy Battery	–/5/3/1	–/+3/+2/+1	Stern/Port/Starboard	4+
Light Battery	–/3/1/–	–/+1/–/–	Bow/Port/Starboard	5+
Point Defense	2/–/–/–	–/–/–/–	All	–
Air Torpedo	4 (Speed 19)	+2	Bow	–

Minotaur Class Armored Cruiser

Class: Minotaur	Category: Cruiser	Armor: 8	Operational Cost: 7	
Speed: 2–7	Altitude: 8	Turns: 2/45	Lift: 1	
Armament	**Firepower**	**Power:**	**Fire Arc**	**Ammo**
Medium Battery	–/4/2/1	–/+2/+1/–	Bow/Port/ Starboard	4+
Medium Battery	–/4/2/1	–/+2/+1/–	Stern/Port/ Starboard	4+
Medium Battery	–/6/3/1	–/+2/+1/–	Port	4+
Medium Battery	–/6/3/1	–/+2/+1/–	Starboard	4+
Point Defense	2/–/–/–	–/–/–/–	All	–

Duke of Edinburgh Class Cruiser

Class: Duke of Edinburgh	Category: Cruiser	Armor: 7	Operational Cost: 4	
Speed: 2–8	Altitude: 8	Turns: 2/45	Lift: 2	
Armament	**Firepower**	**Power**	**Fire Arc**	**Ammo**
Medium Battery	–/6/4/2	–/+2/+1/–	Bow/Port/ Starboard	4+
Medium Battery	–/2/1/–	–/+2/+1/–	Stern/Port/ Starboard	5+
Light Battery	–/8/4/2	–/–/–/–	Port	4+
Light Battery	–/8/4/2	–/–/–/–	Starboard	4+
Point Defense	2/–/–/–	–/–/–/–	All	–

Warrior Class Cruiser

Class: Warrior	Category: Cruiser	Armor: 7	Operational Cost: 4	
Speed: 2–8	Altitude: 8	Turns: 2/45	Lift: 2	
Armament	**Firepower**	**Power**	**Fire Arc**	**Ammo**
Medium Battery	–/3/2/1	–/+3/+2/+1	Bow/Port/ Starboard	4+
Medium Battery	–/3/2/1	–/+3/+2/+1	Stern/Port/ Starboard	4+
Light Battery	–/4/2/–	–/–/–/–	Port	5+
Light Battery	–/4/2/–	–/–/–/–	Starboard	5+
Point Defense	2/–/–/–	–/–/–/–	All	–

Arethusa Class Light Cruiser

Class: Arethusa	Category: Cruiser	Armor: 7	Operational Cost: 4	
Speed: 2–8	Altitude: 9	Turns: 2/45	Lift: 2	
Armament	**Firepower**	**Power**	**Fire Arc**	**Ammo**
Medium Battery	–/2/1/–	–/+2/+1/–	Bow/Port/ Starboard	4+
Medium Battery	–/2/1/–	–/+2/+1/–	Stern/Port/ Starboard	4+
Light Battery	–/3/2/–	–/+2/+1/–	Port	4+
Light Battery	–/3/2/–	–/+2/+1/–	Starboard	4+
Point Defense	2/–/–/–	–/–/–/–	All	–

Active Class Light Cruiser

Class: Active	Category: Cruiser (Light Cruiser)	Armor: 7	Operational Cost: 4	
Speed: 2–10	Altitude: 7	Turns: 2/45	Lift: 2	
Armament	**Firepower**	**Power**	**Fire Arc**	**Ammo**
Medium Battery	–/4/2/1	–/+2/+1/–	Bow/Port/ Starboard	4+
Medium Battery	–/4/2/1	–/+2/+1/–	Stern/Port Starboard	4+
Point Defense	6/–/–/–	–/–/–/–	All	–

Shah Class Frigate

Class: Shah	Category: Escort	Armor: 5	Operational Cost: 5	
Speed: 2–13	Altitude: 9	Turns: 2/45	Lift: 2	
Armament	**Firepower**	**Power**	**Fire Arc**	**Ammo**
Light Battery	–/1/1/–	–/–/–/–	Bow/Port/ Starboard	4+
Point Defense	2/–/–/–	–/–/–/–	All	–
Air Torpedo	2 (Speed 18)	+2	Bow	–

Bull Finch Class Destroyer

Class: Bull Finch	Category: Escort	Armor: 6	Operational Cost: 4	
Speed: 2–12	Altitude: 9	Turns: 2/45	Lift: 2	
Armament	**Firepower**	**Power**	**Fire Arc**	**Ammo**
Light Battery	–/2/1/–	–/–/–/–	Bow/Port/ Starboard	4+
Point Defense	2/–/–/–	–/–/–/–	All	–
Choose *one* of the following weapons:				
Air Torpedo	4 (Speed 18)	+2	Bow	–
Sky Mine	4 (Speed 6)	+2	Stern	–
Bombs	4 (Speed 6)	+2	Stern	–

Lightning Class Torpedo Boat

Class: Lightning	Category: Escort	Armor: 4	Operational Cost: 8	
Speed: 2–14	Altitude: 9	Turns: 2/45	Lift: 3	
Armament	**Firepower**	**Power**	**Fire Arc**	**Ammo**
Point Defense	2/–/–/–	–/–/–/–	All	–
Air Torpedo	1 (Speed 18)	+2	Stern	–

© Brigade Models

French Republic

The forces of the French Republic quickly adopted the new airship technology. Early in the new century *L'Aire Nationale* was formed. The main power of France is based on the continent of Europe. In the past, the French had been the leaders in culture and industry, but the German Empire has been challenging their hold on their position as the pre-eminent power of Europe.

The French are a pragmatic lot and realize the growing power of their German neighbors. As a result, they have been courting alliances with Russia, Italy, and even making overtures to the British. Their major enemies have historically been the British, and the new rising power of Germany.

Like the British, the French were quick to the colonial game with colonies across the globe. They have holdings in the Caribbean, Orient, North Africa, and Southeast Asia. These colonies have been the source of friction with other Great Powers. They have several air fleets scattered at their colonial holdings across the globe.

The French prefer an air strategy focused on harassment and raiding over the Mahan theory of open battle. Therefore, their fleet uses more unconventional arms such as air torpedoes, air mines, and even aeroplanes. They also tend to favor smaller and lighter ships overall.

Command Dice

Determine each captain's Command dice by rolling 1d6 for each ship:

French Republic Command Dice Table	
Roll	**Command dice**
1	1
2–3	2
4–5	3
6	4

French Line of Battle

Courbet Class Battleship				
Class: Courbet	Category: Battleship	Armor: 9	Operational Cost: 11	
Speed: 2–5	Altitude: 7	Turns: 1/45	Lift: 1	
Armament	**Firepower**	**Power**	**Fire Arc**	**Ammo**
Heavy Battery	–/6/4/2	–/+4/+3/+2	Bow/Port/ Starboard	4+
Heavy Battery	–/6/4/2	–/+4/+3/+2	Stern/Port/ Starboard	4+
Medium Battery	–/4/2/–	–/+2/+1/+1	Bow/Port/ Starboard	5+
Medium Battery	–/2/1/–	–/+2/+1/+1	Stern/Port/ Starboard	5+
Point Defense	3/–/–/–	–/–/–/–	All	–
Air Torpedo	4 (Speed 18)	+3	Bow	–

Charles Martel Class Battleship				
Class: Charles Martel	Category: Battleship	Armor: 8	Operational Cost: 6	
Speed: 2–5	Altitude: 7	Turns: 1/45	Lift: 1	
Armament	**Firepower**	**Power**	**Fire Arc**	**Ammo**
Heavy Battery	–/4/3/1	–/+3/+2/+1	Bow/Port/ Starboard	4+
Heavy Battery	–/4/3/1	–/+3/+2/+1	Stern/Port/ Starboard	4+
Medium Battery	–/4/2/–	–/+2/+1/+1	Port	5+
Medium Battery	–/4/2/–	–/+2/+1/+1	Starboard	5+
Light Battery	–/3/1/–	–/+1/–/–	Port	5+
Light battery	–/3/1/–	–/+1/–/–	Starboard	5+
Point Defense	2/–/–/–	–/–/–/–	All	–
Air Torpedo	2 (Speed 18)	+3	Bow	–

Gloire Class Armored Cruiser

Class: Gloire	Category: Cruiser	Armor: 8	Operational Cost: 7	
Speed: 2–5	Altitude: 7	Turns: 2/45	Lift: 2	
Armament	**Firepower**	**Power**	**Fire Arc**	**Ammo**
Heavy Battery	–/3/2/1	–/+2/+2/+1	Bow/Port/ Starboard	4+
Heavy Battery	–/3/2/1	–/+2/+2/+1	Stern/Port/ Starboard	4+
Light Battery	–/2/1/–	–/+1/–/–	Port	5+
Light battery	–/2/1/–	–/+1/–/–	Starboard	5+
Point Defense	3/–/–/–	–/–/–/–	All	–
Air Torpedo	4 (Speed 18)	+3	Bow	–

Descartes Class Cruiser

Class: Descartes	Category: Cruiser	Armor: 7	Operational Cost: 4	
Speed: 2–8	Altitude: 7	Turns: 2/45	Lift: 2	
Armament	**Firepower**	**Power**	**Fire Arc**	**Ammo**
Medium Battery	–/3/2/1	–/+2/+1/–	Bow/Port	5+
Medium Battery	–/3/2/1	–/+2/+1/–	Bow/ Starboard	5+
Light Battery	–/3/1/–	–/+1/–/–	Bow	5+
Light battery	–/3/1/–	–/+1/–/–	Stern	5+
Point Defense	2/–/–/–	–/–/–/–	All	–
Air Torpedo	2 (Speed 18)	+3	Bow	–
Bombs	4 (Speed 6)	+1	Stern	–

D'Iberville Class Cruiser

Class: D'Iberville	Category: Cruiser	Armor: 7	Operational Cost: 4	
Speed: 2–8	Altitude: 7	Turns: 2/45	Lift: 2	
Armament	Firepower	Power	Fire Arc	Ammo
Light Battery	–/3/1/–	–/+1/–/–	Bow	5+
Light battery	–/3/1/–	–/+1/–/–	Stern	5+
Point Defense	3/–/–/–	–/–/–/–	All	–
Air Torpedo	3 (Speed 18)	+3	Bow/Port	–
Air Torpedo	3 (Speed 18)	+3	Bow/Starboard	–

Foudre Class Cruiser

Class: Foudre	Category: Cruiser	Armor: 7	Operational Cost: 4	
Speed: 2–8	Altitude: 7	Turns: 2/45	Lift: 2	
Armament	**Firepower**	**Power**	**Fire Arc**	**Ammo**
Point Defense	4/–/–/–	–/–/–/–	All	–
Air Torpedo	2 (Speed 18)	+3	Bow	–
Sky Mines	4 (Speed 6)	+2	Stern	–
Aeroplanes	2 (Speed 10)	+3	Port/Starboard	–

Chasseur Class Destroyer

Class: Chasseur	Category: Escort	Armor: 6	Operational Cost: 3	
Speed: 2–10	Altitude: 9	Turns: 2/45	Lift: 2	
Armament	**Firepower**	**Power**	**Fire Arc**	**Ammo**
Light Battery	–/3/1/–	–/+1/–/–	Bow	5+
Point Defense	2/–/–/–	–/–/–/–	All	–
Choose *one* of the following weapons				
Air Torpedo	3 (Speed 18)	+3	Bow	–
Sky Mine	4 (Speed 6)	+2	Stern	–

German Empire

The German Imperial Navy has spent millions of marks and thousands of man-hours to challenge the British Royal Navy's mastery of the skies. Once the British launched their first airship, Germany spotted an opportunity to equal the British forces. They bent all of their growing industrial and scientific effort to build their own air fleet.

The Germans had a later start than the British or French in the race for colonies and they are eager to catch up. However, some of their early ambition was thwarted by the British and the French, leading to bitter German resentment. These events spurred the German Government to build their own airship fleet.

The German Empire has a natural alliance with the Austro-Hungarian Empire. They have close geographic, linguistic, and historical ties. They also have good relations with the Ottoman Turks and the United States. Their natural rivals are the British, Russians, and French.

Command Dice

Determine each captain's Command dice by rolling 1d6 for each ship:

German Empire Command Dice Table	
Roll	Command dice
1	1
2–3	2
4–5	3
6	4

German Line of Battle

Nassau Class Battleship				
Class: Nassau	Category: Battleship	Armor: 9	Operational Cost: 12	
Speed: 2–5	Altitude: 7	Turns: 1/90	Lift: 1	
Armament	Firepower	Power	Fire Arc	Ammo
Heavy Battery	–/7/5/3	–/+3/+2/+1	Bow/Port/ Starboard	3+
Heavy Battery	–/5/3/1	–/+3/+2/+1	Stern/Port/ Starboard	3+
Light Battery	–/3/1/–	–/+1/–/–	Bow/Port/ Starboard	4+
Light Battery	–/3/1/–	–/+1/–/–	Stern/Port/Starboard	4+
Point Defense	2/–/–/–	–/–/–/–	All	–
Air Torpedo	1 (Speed 18)	+3	Bow	–
Air Torpedo	2 (Speed 18)	+3	Port/Starboard	–

Deutschland Class Heavy Cruiser				
Class: Deutschland	Category: Battleship	Armor: 8	Operational Cost: 6	
Speed: 2–5	Altitude: 7	Turns: 1/45	Lift: 1	
Armament	Firepower	Power	Fire Arc	Ammo
Heavy Battery	–/4/3/1	–/+3/+2/+1	Bow/Port/ Starboard	3+
Heavy Battery	–/4/3/1	–/+3/+2/+1	Stern/Port/ Starboard	3+
Medium Battery	–/4/2/–	–/+2/+1/–	Bow/Port/ Starboard	4+
Medium Battery	–/4/2/–	–/+2/+1/–	Stern/Port/ Starboard	4+
Light Battery	–/3/1/–	–/+1/–/–	Bow/Port/ Starboard	4+
Light Battery	–/3/1/–	–/+1/–/–	Stern/Port/ Starboard	4+
Point Defense	2/–/–/–	–/–/–/–	All	–

Derfflinger Class Battlecruiser

Class: Derfflinger	Category: Cruiser	Armor: 8	Operational Cost: 7	
Speed: 2–6	Altitude: 8	Turns: 1/90	Lift: 1	
Armament	**Firepower**	**Power**	**Fire Arc**	**Ammo**
Heavy Battery	–/4/2/1	–/+3/+2/+1	Bow/Port/Starboard	3+
Heavy Battery	–/4/2/1	–/+3/+2/+1	Stern/Port/Starboard	3+
Light Battery	–/4/2/–	–/–/–/–	Bow/Starboard	4+
Light Battery	–/4/2/–	–/–/–/–	Bow/Port	4+
Point Defense	2/–/–/–	–/–/–/–	All	–
Air Torpedo	1 (Speed 18)	+3	Bow	–
Air Torpedo	2 (Speed 18)	+3	Port/Starboard	–

Scharnhorst Class Armored Cruiser

Class: Scharnhorst	Category: Cruiser	Armor: 8	Operational Cost: 7	
Speed: 2–7	Altitude: 8	Turns: 2/45	Lift: 1	
Armament	**Firepower**	**Power**	**Fire Arc**	**Ammo**
Medium Battery	–/4/2/1	–/+2/+1/–	Bow/Port/Starboard	3+
Medium Battery	–/4/2/1	–/+2/+1/–	Stern/Port/Starboard	3+
Medium Battery	–/4/2/1	–/+2/+1/–	Port	4+
Medium Battery	–/4/2/1	–/+2/+1/–	Starboard	4+
Light Battery	–/3/2/1	–/–/–/–	Port	4+
Light Battery	–/3/2/1	–/–/–/–	Starboard	4+
Point Defense	2/–/–/–	–/–/–/–	All	–
Air Torpedo	1 (Speed 18)	+3	Bow	–
Bombs	6 (Speed 6)	+1	Stern	–

Magdeburg Class Light Cruiser

Class: Magdeburg	Category: Cruiser	Armor: 7	Operational Cost: 4	
Speed: 2–8	Altitude: 9	Turns: 2/45	Lift: 2	
Armament	**Firepower**	**Power**	**Fire Arc**	**Ammo**
Medium Battery	–/2/1/–	–/+2/+1/–	Bow/Port/Starboard	3+
Medium Battery	–/2/1/–`	–/+2/+1/–	Stern/Port/Starboard	3+
Light Battery	–/3/2/–	–/+2/+1/–	Port	4+
Light Battery	–/3/2/–	–/+2/+1/–	Starboard	4+
Point Defense	2/–/–/–	–/–/–/–	All	–
Bombs	4 (Speed 6)	+1	Stern	–

S-Class Destroyer

Class: S-Class	Category: Escort	Armor: 6	Operational Cost: 4	
Speed: 2–12	Altitude: 9	Turns: 1/90	Lift: 2	
Armament	**Firepower**	**Power**	**Fire Arc**	**Ammo**
Light Battery	–/2/1/–	–/–/–/–	Bow/Port/Starboard	3+
Point Defense	2/–/–/–	–/–/–/–	All	–
Choose *one* of the following weapons				
Sky Mine	4 (Speed 6)	+2	Stern	–
Bombs	4 (Speed 6)	+1	Stern	–
Air Torpedo	4 (Speed 18)	+2	Bow	–

G-Class Torpedo Boat

Class: G-Class	Category: Escort	Armor: 4	Operational Cost: 9	
Speed: 2–14	Altitude: 9	Turns: 2/90	Lift: 3	
Armament	**Firepower**	**Power**	**Fire Arc**	**Ammo**
Point Defense	2/–/–/–	–/–/–/–	All	–
Air Torpedo	2 (Speed 18)	+2	Stern	–

Russian Empire

The Russian Empire is the largest in pure size and population. The Russians were late to the airship revolution, and they have consistently had design and development problems since their attempts at building an air navy commenced two decades ago. However, despite these setbacks the Russians have a fleet in being that is deployed across the great bulk of their nation. The fleet itself is split between major bases in the Ukraine, the Black Sea, and along the Pacific coast. It has only a token presence elsewhere in the Empire.

The Russian Empire is a restless and hungry beast. Despite the vast tracts of undeveloped land, it is constantly pushing outwards. The Czar of Russia is a fervent believer in Pan-Slavism and seeks to unite all Slavic people under the Russian banner. Therefore, they are natural enemies of the Austro-Hungarians. They have also repeatedly encroached on Ottoman territory, attempting to gain access to the Mediterranean Sea. To their south they play the great game with Britain for a sphere of Influence on the northwestern edge of India. Finally, they impinge on the Japanese sphere of influence in China and Asia.

The Russian Empire has many enemies and few friends. However, they have managed to court the French, who fear growing German power in Europe. The Italians are also friendly to the Russians, as they have a mutual enemy in the Austro-Hungarians and Ottomans.

Command Dice

Determine each captain's Command dice by rolling 1d6 for each ship:

Russian Empire Command Dice Table	
Roll	**Command dice**
1–2	1
3–4	2
5	3
6	4

Russian Line of Battle

Imperatrista Mariya Class Battleship

Class: Imperatrista Mariya	Category: Battleship	Armor: 8	Operational Cost: 6	
Speed: 1–5	Altitude: 7	Turns: 1/45	Lift: 1	
Armament	**Firepower**	**Power**	**Fire Arc**	**Ammo**
Heavy Battery	–/5/3/2	–/+4/+3/+2	Bow/Port/ Starboard	4+
Heavy Battery	–/5/3/2	–/+4/+3/+2	Stern/Port/ Starboard	4+
Medium Battery	–/4/2/–	–/+2/+1/+1	Bow/Port/ Starboard	5+
Medium Battery	–/2/1/–	–/+2/+1/+1	Stern/Port/ Starboard	5+
Point Defense	3/–/–/–	–/–/–/–	All	–
Air Torpedo	2 (Speed 18)	+3	Bow	–

Bayan Class Cruiser

Class: Bayan	Category: Cruiser	Armor: 7	Operational Cost: 4	
Speed: 1–6	Altitude: 7	Turns: 2/45	Lift: 2	
Armament	**Firepower**	**Power**	**Fire Arc**	**Ammo**
Medium Battery	–/3/2/1	–/+2/+1/–	Bow/Port/ Starboard	5+
Medium Battery	–/3/2/1	–/+2/+1/–	Stern/Port/ Starboard	5+
Point Defense	3/–/–/–	–/–/–/–	All	–
Air Torpedo	2 (Speed 18)	+2	Bow	–
Sky Mines	4 (Speed 6)	+2	Stern	–
Bombs	4 (Speed 6)	+1	Stern	–

Bogatyr Class Cruiser

Class: Bogatyr	Category: Cruiser	Armor: 7	Operational Cost: 3	
Speed: 1–6	Altitude: 7	Turns: 2/45	Lift: 1	
Armament	**Firepower**	**Power**	**Fire Arc:**	**Ammo**
Medium Battery	–/4/2/1	–/+2/+1/–	Bow/Port/ Starboard	4+
Medium Battery	–/4/2/1	–/+2/+1/–	Stern/Port/ Starboard	4+
Light Battery	–/4/2/–	–/+1/–/–	Port	5+
Light Battery	–/4/2/–	–/+1/–/–	Starboard	5+
Point Defense	3/–/–/–	–/–/– /–	All	–
Air Torpedo	2 (Speed 18)	+2	Bow	–

Izyaslav Class Destroyer

Class: Izyaslav	Category: Escort	Armor: 6	Operational Cost: 4	
Speed: 1–10	Altitude: 9	Turns: 2/45	Lift: 2	
Armament	**Firepower**	**Power**	**Fire Arc**	**Ammo**
Light Battery	–/2/1/–	–/–/–/–	Bow/Port/ Starboard	5+
Point Defense	2/–/–/–	–/–/–/–	All	–
Choose *one* of the following weapons				
Air Torpedo	3 (Speed 18)	+2	Bow	–
Sky Mines	4 (Speed 6)	+2	Stern	–
Bombs	4 (Speed 18)	+1	Stern	–

Krasnoye Class Gunboat

Class: Krasnoye	Category: Escort	Armor: 5	Operational Cost: 4	
Speed: 1–5	Altitude: 7	Turns: 2/45	Lift: 2	
Armament	**Firepower**	**Power**	**Fire Arc**	**Ammo**
Light Battery	–/4/1/–	–/+1/–/–	Bow/Port/ Starboard	5+
Point Defense	1	–/–/–/–	All	–
Sky Mines	2 (Speed 6)	+2	Stern	–

Austro-Hungarian Empire

The Austro-Hungarian Empire is one of the oldest powers in Europe. The ruling Habsburg family has been political players since the Middle Ages. Over that time, their Empire had waxed but is now considered by many to be on the wane. It is often referred to as the Old Man of Europe.

Unlike other nations, the Dual Monarchy is co-ruled by the Austrian Habsburgs and their Hungarian counterparts. This has led to a peculiar arrangement with two parliaments and other oddities. Besides the divide between the Germanic Austrians and the Slavic Hungarians, the rest of the Empire is a mixture of ethnicities, many speaking different languages and all with unique customs.

Unsurprisingly, this has led to many difficulties when building, maintaining, and deploying the new technology of airships. The Austro-Hungarians were late to the party, but nevertheless saw the importance of creating such a fleet. Protection of their national interests in the Mediterranean and Balkans make the fleet vital.

The Austro-Hungarians are close allies with Germany; they also have ties to Russia and the British. However, the Tsar of Russia's fascination with Pan-Slavism has led to tensions between the two powers. Their traditional enemies are the Ottoman Empire and the French, but relations with both countries are improving. Their mortal enemy is the Kingdom of Italy, which covets the Dual Monarchy's lands in the Adriatic.

Command Dice

Determine each captain's Command dice by rolling 1d6 for each ship:

Austro-Hungarian Command Dice Table	
Roll	Command dice
1	1
2–3	2
4–5	3
6	4

Austro-Hungarian Line of Battle

Tegetthoff Class Battleship				
Class: Tegetthoff	Category: Battleship	Armor: 9	Operational Cost: 11	
Speed: 2–5	Altitude: 7	Turns: 1/45	Lift: 1	
Armament	Firepower	Power	Fire Arc	Ammo
Heavy Battery	–/6/4/2	–/+4/+3/+2	Bow/Port/ Starboard	4+
Heavy Battery	–/6/4/2	–/+4/+3/+2	Stern/Port/Starboard	4+
Medium Battery	–/4/2/–	–/+2/+1/–	Bow/Port/ Starboard	5+
Medium Battery	–/4/2/–	–/+2/+1/–	Stern/Port/Starboard	5+
Point Defense	3/–/–/–	–/–/–/–	All	–
Air Torpedo	4 (Speed 18)	+3	Bow	–

Erzhog Karl Class Heavy Cruiser				
Class: Erzhog Karl	Category: Battleship	Armor: 8	Operational Cost: 6	
Speed: 2–5	Altitude: 7	Turns: 1/45	Lift: 1	
Armament	Firepower	Power	Fire Arc	Ammo
Heavy Battery	–/4/3/1	–/+3/+2/+1	Bow/Port/Starboard	4+
Heavy Battery	–/4/3/1	–/+3/+2/+1	Stern/Port/Starboard	4+
Medium Battery	–/4/2/–	–/+2/+1/–	Port	5+
Medium Battery	–/4/2/–	–/+2/+1/–	Starboard	5+
Light Battery	–/3/1/–	–/+1/–/–	Port	5+
Light Battery	–/3/1/–	–/+1/–/–	Starboard	5+
Point Defense	3/–/–/–	–/–/–/–	All	–
Air Torpedo	3 (Speed 18)	+3	Bow	–

Kaiserin Class Armored Cruiser

Class: Kaiserin	Category: Cruiser	Armor: 8	Operational Cost: 7	
Speed: 2–7	Altitude: 8	Turns: 2/45	Lift: 2	
Armament	**Firepower**	**Power**	**Fire Arc**	**Ammo**
Medium Battery	–/3/2/1	–/+2/+1/–	Bow/Port/Starboard	4+
Medium Battery	–/3/2/1	–/+2/+1/–	Stern/Port/Starboard	4+
Light Battery	–/2/1/–	–/+1/–/–	Port	5+
Light Battery	–/2/1/–	–/+1/–/–	Starboard	5+
Point Defense	3/–/–/–	–/–/–/–	All	–
Air Torpedo	4 (Speed 18)	+3	Bow	–
Bombs	4 (Speed 6)	+1	Stern	–

Zenta Class Cruiser

Class: Zenta	Category: Cruiser	Armor: 7	Operational Cost: 4	
Speed: 2–8	Altitude: 8	Turns: 2/45	Lift: 2	
Armament	**Firepower**	**Power**	**Fire Arc**	**Ammo**
Medium Battery	–/3/2/1	–/+2/+1/–	Bow/Port	5+
Medium Battery	–/3/2/1	–/+2/+1/–	Bow/ Starboard	5+
Light Battery	–/3/1/–	–/+1/–/–	Bow	5+
Light Battery	–/3/1/–	–/+1/–/–	Stern	5+
Point Defense	2/–/–/–	–/–/–/–	All	–
Air Torpedo	2 (Speed 18)	+3	Bow	–

Novara Class Cruiser

Class: Novara	Category: Cruiser	Armor: 7	Operational Cost: 4	
Speed: 2–9	Altitude: 8	Turns: 2/45	Lift: 2	
Armament	**Firepower**	**Power**	**Fire Arc**	**Ammo**
Light Battery	–/3/1/–	–/+1/–/–	Bow	5+
Light Battery	–/3/1/–	–/+1/–/–	Stern	5+
Point Defense	3/–/–/–	–/–/–/–	All	–
Air Torpedo	6 (Speed 18)	+3	Bow	–

Huzsar Class Destroyer

Class: Huzsar	Category: Escort	Armor: 6	Operational Cost: 3	
Speed: 2–10	Altitude: 9	Turns: 2/45	Lift: 2	
Armament	**Firepower**	**Power**	**Fire Arc**	**Ammo**
Light Battery	–/3/1/–	–/+1/–/–	Bow/Port/Starboard	5+
Point Defense	2/–/–/–	–/–/–/–	All	–
Choose *one* of the following weapons				
Air Torpedo	3 (Speed 18)	+2	Bow	–
Sky Mine	4 (Speed 6)	+2	Bow	–

Kingdom of Italy

The Kingdom of Italy is a relatively new player on the European scene. The Italians have founded colonies in North Africa and the Horn of Africa, wresting these lands away from the Ottoman Empire. In addition, Italian eyes have been locked on the far side of the Adriatic and the Italian-speaking minorities in Austro-Hungarian territory.

Italians have been sailing the Mediterranean for centuries. As such they have a strong familiarity with the region, and their air fleets are primarily concerned with it. However, they have also been sighted in Africa, the Red Sea, and around the Alps.

The Italians have few strong allies. However, they are clearly foes and rivals of Austro-Hungarians and Ottomans.

Command Dice

Determine each captain's Command dice by rolling 1d6 for each ship:

Kingdom of Italy Command Dice Table	
Roll	Command dice
1	1
2–4	2
5	3
6	4

Italian Order of Battle

Conti di Cavour Class Battleship					
Class: Conti di Cavour	Category: Battleship	Armor: 9	Operational Cost: 11		
Speed: 2–7	Altitude: 7	Turns: 1/45	Lift: 1		
Armament	**Firepower**	**Power**	**Fire Arc**	**Ammo**	
Heavy Battery	–/9/6/3	–/+4/+3/+2	Bow/Port/Starboard	4+	
Heavy Battery	–/6/4/2	–/+4/+3/+2	Stern/Port/Starboard	4+	
Light Battery	–/2/1/–	–/+1/–/–	Bow/Port/Starboard	5+	
Light Battery	–/2/1/–	–/+1/–/–	Stern/Port/Starboard	5+	
Point Defense	2/–/–/–	–/–/–/–	All	–	
Air Torpedo	2 (Speed 18)	+3	Bow	–	
Air Torpedo	1 (Speed 18)	+3	Stern	–	

Vettor Pisani Class Armored Cruiser

Class: Vettor Pisani	Category: Cruiser	Armor: 8	Operational Cost: 7	
Speed: 2–6	Altitude: 8	Turns: 2/45	Lift: 2	
Armament	**Firepower**	**Power**	**Fire Arc**	**Ammo**
Medium Battery	–/4/2/1	–/+2/+1/–	Port	4+
Medium Battery	–/4/2/1	–/+2/+1/–	Starboard	4+
Light Battery	–/2/1/–	–/+1/–/–	Port	5+
Light Battery	–/2/1/–	–/+1/–/–	Starboard	5+
Point Defense	3/–/–/–	–/–/–/–	All	–
Air Torpedo	4 (Speed 18)	+3	Bow	–

Garibaldi Class Cruiser

Class: Garibaldi	Category: Cruiser	Armor: 7	Operational Cost: 4	
Speed: 2–8	Altitude: 8	Turns: 2/45	Lift: 2	
Armament	**Firepower**	**Power**	**Fire Arc**	**Ammo**
Medium Battery	–/3/2/1	–/+2/+1/–	Bow/Port	5+
Medium Battery	–/3/2/1	–/+2/+1/–	Bow/Starboard	5+
Light Battery	–/3/1/–	–/+1/–/–	Bow	5+
Light Battery	–/3/1/–	–/+1/–/–	Stern	5+
Point Defense	2/–/–/–	–/–/–/–	All	–
Air Torpedo	2 (Speed 18)	+3	Bow	–

Piedmonte Class Cruiser

Class: Piedmonte	Category: Cruiser	Armor: 7	Operational Cost: 4	
Speed: 2–6	Altitude: 8	Turns: 2/45	Lift: 2	
Armament	**Firepower**	**Power**	**Fire Arc**	**Ammo**
Medium Battery	–/3/2/1	–/+2/+1/–	Bow/Port	5+
Medium Battery	–/3/2/1	–/+2/+1/–	Bow/Starboard	5+
Light Battery	–/3/1/–	–/+1/–/–	Bow	5+
Light Battery	–/3/1/–	–/+1/–/–	Stern	5+
Point Defense	2/–/–/–	–/–/–/–	All	–
Air Torpedo	2 (Speed 18)	+2	Bow	–
Bombs	4 (Speed 6)	+1	Stern	–

Soldato Class Frigate

Class: Soldato	Category: Escort	Armor: 5	Operational Cost: 5	
Speed: 2–12	Altitude: 9	Turns: 2/45	Lift: 2	
Armament	**Firepower**	**Power**	**Fire Arc**	**Ammo**
Light Battery	–/1/1/–	–/–/–/–	Bow/Port/Starboard	4+
Point Defense	2/–/–/–	–/–/–/–	All	–
Air Torpedo	2 (Speed 18)	+2	Bow	–

Turbine Class Destroyer

Class: Turbine	Category: Escort	Armor: 6	Operational Cost: 3	
Speed: 2–10	Altitude: 9	Turns: 2/45	Lift: 2	
Armament	**Firepower**	**Power**	**Fire Arc**	**Ammo**
Light Battery	–/2/1/–	–/+1/–/–	Bow/Port/Starboard	5+
Point Defense	2/–/–/–	–/–/–/–	All	–
Air Torpedo	3 (Speed 18)	+2	Bow	–
Sky Mine	4 (Speed 6)	+2	Bow	–

Pilo Class Torpedo Boat

Class: Pilo	Category: Escort	Armor: 4	Operational Cost: 8	
Speed: 2–14	Altitude: 9	Turns: 2/45	Lift: 3	
Armament	**Firepower**	**Power**	**Fire Arc**	**Ammo**
Point Defense	2/–/–/–	–/–/–/–	All	–
Air Torpedo	1 (Speed 18)	+2	Stern	–

United States of America

The vast size of the United States and its rugged terrain means that the new nation quickly adopted the airship as means of commerce and transport. The United States Navy, however, was slower to modernize to the new technology.

The United States has colonies in the Pacific and claims a sphere of influence in the Western Hemisphere. However, France, Britain, and Germany all have their own influence in the region. The United States can do little to expel them from the region, and the talk of the Monroe Doctrine is mostly bluster.

The United States has few rivalries compared to other growing Great Powers. However, they have come into conflict with Russia and Japan in the Pacific and have had tensions with the British and French in South America and the Caribbean. Germany has also been getting into the mix in South America.

Command Dice

Determine each captain's Command dice by rolling 1d6 for each ship:

United States Command Dice Table	
Roll	Command dice
1	1
2–4	2
5	3
6	4

United States Order of Battle

Michigan Class Battleship					
Class: Michigan	Category: Battleship	Armor: 9		Operational Cost: 11	
Speed: 2–5	Altitude: 7	Turns: 1/45		Lift: 1	
Armament	**Firepower**	**Power**		**Fire Arc**	**Ammo**
Heavy Battery	–/5/3/1	–/+4/+2/+1		Bow/Port/Starboard	4+
Heavy Battery	–/5/3/1	–/+4/+2/+1		Stern/Port/Starboard	4+
Medium Battery	–/4/3/1	–/+2/+1/–		Bow/Port/Starboard	5+
Medium Battery	–/3/2/1	–/+2/+1/–		Stern/Port/Starboard	5+
Point Defense	2/–/–/–	–/–/–/–		All	–

Connecticut Class Heavy Cruiser					
Class: Connecticut	Category: Battleship	Armor: 8		Operational Cost: 6	
Speed: 2–5	Altitude: 7	Turns: 1/45		Lift: 1	
Armament	**Firepower**	**Power**		**Fire Arc**	**Ammo**
Heavy Battery	–/4/3/1	–/+3/+2/+1		Bow/Port/Starboard	4+
Heavy Battery	–/4/3/1	–/+3/+2/+1		Stern/Port/Starboard	4+
Medium Battery	–/4/2/–	–/+2/+1/–		Port	5+
Medium Battery	–/4/2/–	–/+2/+1/–		Starboard	5+
Light Battery	–/4/3/1	–/–/–/–		Port	5+
Light Battery	–/3/2/1	–/–/–/–		Starboard	5+
Point Defense	2/–/–/–	–/–/–/–		All	–

Tennessee Class Armored Cruiser					
Class: Tennessee	Category: Cruiser	Armor: 8		Operational Cost: 7	
Speed: 2–6	Altitude: 8	Turns: 2/45		Lift: 1	
Armament	**Firepower**	**Power**		**Fire Arc**	**Ammo**
Medium Battery	–/4/2/1	–/+2/+1/–		Bow/Port/Starboard	4+
Medium Battery	–/4/2/1	–/+2/+1/–		Stern/Port/Starboard	4+
Medium Battery	–/6/3/1	–/+2/+1/–		Port	5+
Medium Battery	–/6/3/1	–/+2/+1/–		Starboard	5+
Point Defense	1/–/–/–	–/–/–/–		All	–
Bombs	6 (Speed 6)	+1		Stern	–

Denver Class Cruiser

Class: Denver	Category: Cruiser	Armor: 7	Operational Cost: 6	
Speed: 2–7	Altitude: 8	Turns: 2/45	Lift: 2	
Armament	**Firepower**	**Power**	**Fire Arc**	**Ammo**
Medium Battery	–/3/2/–	–/+3/+2/–	Bow/Port/Starboard	4+
Medium Battery	–/3/2/–	–/+3/+2/–1	Stern/Port/Starboard	4+
Light Battery	–/4/2/–	–/–/–/–	Port	5+
Light Battery	–/4/2/–	–/–/–/–	Starboard	5+
Point Defense	2/–/–/–	–/–/–/–	All	–
Bombs	4 (Speed 6)	+1	Stern	–

Chester Class Light Cruiser

Class: Chester	Category: Cruiser	Armor: 7	Operational Cost: 4	
Speed: 2–9	Altitude: 9	Turns: 2/45	Lift: 2	
Armament	**Firepower**	**Power**	**Fire Arc**	**Ammo**
Medium Battery	–/2/1/–	–/+2/+1/–	Bow/Port/Starboard	4+
Medium Battery	–/2/1/–	–/+2/+1/–	Stern/Port/Starboard	4+
Point Defense	2/–/–/–	–/–/–/–	All	–
Aeroplanes	1 (Speed 10)		Stern	–

Bainbridge Class Destroyer

Class: Bainbridge	Category: Escort	Armor: 6	Operational Cost: 3	
Speed: 2–10	Altitude: 9	Turns: 2/45	Lift: 2	
Armament	**Firepower**	**Power**	**Fire Arc**	**Ammo**
Light Battery	–/2/1/–	–/+1/–/–	Bow/Port/Starboard	4+
Point Defense	2/–/–/–	–/–/–/–	All	–
Choose *one* of the following weapons				
Sky Mine	4 (Speed 6)	+2	Stern	–
Air Torpedo	4 (Speed 18)	+2	Bow	–

Empire of Japan

The Japanese have decided to modernize in the face of Western power, abandoning their previous reluctance and fully adopting many Western practices. The development and building of the air navy is no exception.

The Japanese wish to carve out their own sphere of influence in the Pacific and the edge of Asia. For the most part, they have allied with the British as a means to this end. They have established nearby colonies in Korea, Manchuria, and various Pacific Island chains.

The Japanese are close allies of the British. However, they have had growing tensions with the United States, Russia, and Germany. They are confident in their powerful air navy and are not afraid of their Great Power rivals. The Japanese Empire is an up-and-coming Power in the Pacific.

Command Dice

Determine each captain's Command dice by rolling 1d6 for each ship:

Empire of Japan Command Dice Table	
Roll	Command dice
1	1
2–3	2
4–5	3
6	4

Japanese Order of Battle

Kawachi Class Battleship

Class: Kawachi	Category: Battleship	Armor: 9	Operational Cost: 11	
Speed: 2–5	Altitude: 7	Turns: 1/45	Lift: 1	
Armament	**Firepower**	**Power**	**Fire Arc**	**Ammo**
Heavy Battery	–/7/5/3	–/+3/+2/+1	Bow/Port/Starboard	4+
Heavy Battery	–/7/5/3	–/+3/+2/+1	Stern/Port/Starboard	4+
Light Battery	–/3/1/–	–/+1/–/–	Port	4+
Light Battery	–/3/1/–	–/+1/–/–	Starboard	4+
Point Defense	2/–/–/–	–/–/–/–	All	–
Air Torpedo	1 (speed 18)	+3	Bow/Stern	–
Air Torpedo	1 (Speed 18)	+3	Port/Starboard	–

Satsuma Class Heavy Cruiser

Class: Satsuma	Category: Battleship	Armor: 8	Operational Cost: 6	
Speed: 2–5	Altitude: 7	Turns: 1/45	Lift: 1	
Armament	**Firepower**	**Power**	**Fire Arc**	**Ammo**
Heavy Battery	–/4/3/1	–/+3/+2/+1	Bow/Port/Starboard	4+
Heavy Battery	–/4/2/1	–/+2/+1/+1	Stern/Port/Starboard	4+
Medium Battery	–/4/2/–	–/+2/+1/–	Port	4+
Medium Battery	–/4/2/–	–/+2/+1/–	Starboard	4+
Light Battery	–/3/1/–	–/–/–/–	Port	4+
Light Battery	–/3/1/–	–/–/–/–	Starboard	4+
Point Defense	2/–/–/–	–/–/–/–	All	–
Air Torpedo	1 (speed 18)	+3	Stern	–
Air Torpedo	2 (Speed 18)	+3	Port/Starboard	–

Kasuga Class Armored Cruiser

Class: Kasuga	Category: Cruiser	Armor: 8	Operational Cost: 7	
Speed: 2–6	Altitude: 8	Turns: 2/45	Lift: 2	
Armament	**Firepower**	**Power**	**Fire Arc**	**Ammo**
Medium Battery	–/4/2/1	–/+2/+1/–	Port	4+
Medium Battery	–/4/2/1	–/+2/+1/–	Starboard	4+
Light Battery	–/2/1/–	–/+1/–/–	Port	4+
Light Battery	–/2/1/–	–/+1/–/–	Starboard	4+
Point Defense	3/–/–/–	–/–/–/–	All	–
Air Torpedo	4 (Speed 18)	+3	Bow	–

Kongo Class Battlecruiser

Class: Kongo	Category: Cruiser	Armor: 7	Operational Cost: 6	
Speed: 2–8	Altitude: 8	Turns: 1/45	Lift: 1	
Armament	**Firepower**	**Power**	**Fire Arc**	**Ammo**
Heavy Battery	–/5/3/1	–/+3/+2/+1	Bow/Port/Starboard	4+
Heavy Battery	–/5/3/1	–/+3/+2/+1	Stern/Port/Starboard	4+
Medium Battery	–/4/3/2	–/+2/+1/–	Port/ Starboard	4+
Point Defense	2/–/–/–	–/–/–/–	All	–
Air Torpedo	4 (speed 18)	+3	Port	–
Air Torpedo	4 (Speed 18)	+3	Starboard	–

Tsushima Class Cruiser

Class: Tsushima	Category: Cruiser	Armor: 7	Operational Cost: 4	
Speed: 2–6	Altitude: 8	Turns: 2/45	Lift: 2	
Armament	**Firepower**	**Power**	**Fire Arc**	**Ammo**
Light Battery	–/3/2/1	–/+1/–/–	Bow/Port	4+
Light Battery	–/3/2/1	–/+1/–/–	Bow/Starboard	4+

Armament	Firepower	Power	Fire Arc	Ammo
Light Battery	–/3/1/–	–/+1/–/–	Port	4+
Light Battery	–/3/1/–	–/+1/–/–	Starboard	4+
Point Defense	2/–/–/–	–/–/–/–	All	–
Air Torpedo	2 (Speed 18)	+2	Bow	–
Bombs	4 (Speed 6)	+1	Stern	–

Yodo Class Light Cruiser

Class: Yodo	Category: Cruiser	Armor: 7	Operational Cost: 4	
Speed: 2–8	Altitude: 9	Turns: 2/45	Lift: 2	
Armament	**Firepower**	**Power**	**Fire Arc**	**Ammo**
Medium Battery	–/2/1/–	–/+2/+1/–	Bow/Port/Starboard	4+
Medium Battery	–/2/1/–	–/+2/+1/–	Bow/Port/Starboard	4+
Light Battery	–/3/2/–	–/+2/+1/–	Port	4+
Light Battery	–/3/2/–	–/+2/+1/–	Starboard	4+
Point Defense	2/–/–/–	–/–/–/–	All	–
Bombs	4 (Speed 6)	+1	Stern	–

Wakamiya Class Light Cruiser

Class: Wakamiya	Category: Cruiser	Armor: 7	Operational Cost: 4	
Speed: 2–8	Altitude: 7	Turns: 2/45	Lift: 2	
Armament	**Firepower**	**Power**	**Fire Arc**	**Ammo**
Point Defense	4/–/–/–	–/–/–/–	All	–
Air Torpedo	2 (Speed 18)	+3	Bow	–
Sky Mines	4 (Speed 6)	+2	Stern	–
Aeroplanes	2 (Speed 10)	+3	Port/Starboard	–

Sakura Class Destroyer

Class: Sakura	Category: Escort	Armor: 6	Operational Cost: 4	
Speed: 2–10	Altitude: 9	Turns: 2/45	Lift: 2	
Armament	**Firepower**	**Power**	**Fire Arc**	**Ammo**
Light Battery	–/2/1/–	–/+1/–/–	Bow/Port/Starboard	4+
Point Defense	2/–/–/–	–/–/–/–	All	–
Air Torpedo	3 (Speed 18)	+2	Bow	–
Sky Mine	4 (Speed 6)	+1	Stern	–

Ottoman Empire

The Ottoman Empire was a notable threat and rival to all the Central European powers throughout the Renaissance and Enlightenment. They continue to hang onto parts of the Balkans and Middle East but have lost sizeable areas of their former domain. Most European powers see the Ottomans as a 'sick man' and are waiting for them to collapse, but they are still a force to be reckoned with.

The Ottoman Court itself has been attempting to modernize its own infrastructure and army. However, it is a conservative nation and many in the court of the Sultan view such reforms and westernization with suspicion. This has slowed their development of an Air Navy.

Most of the Sultan's Air Fleet are foreign purchased ships. The production facilities of the Empire themselves are not sufficient to build Airships but are capable of maintaining them. Therefore, the Sultan's fleets are made up of a variety of vessels from shipyards of various Great Powers.

© Brigade Models

The Ottoman's have no solid allies as each Great Power will support and oppose them as their fickle whims demand. However, they are most likely to come into conflict with the Austro-Hungarians, Russians, and Italians. The French, Germans, and the British vacillate between apathy and support.

Determining Command Dice

Ottoman Command Dice Table	
D6 Roll	**Command Dice**
1	1
2–4	2
5-6	3

Ottoman Line of Battle

Sultan Osmann-I Evvel Class Battleship				
Class: Sultan Osmann-I Evvel	Category: Battleship	Armor: 9	Operational Cost: 11	
Speed: 2–6	Altitude: 7	Turns: 1/45	Lift: 1	
Armament	**Firepower**	**Power**	**Fire Arc**	**Ammo**
Heavy Battery	–/5/3/1	–/+4/+2/+1	Bow/Port/Starboard	5+
Heavy Battery	–/5/3/1	–/+4/+2/+1	Stern/Port/Starboard	5+
Light Battery	–/4/3/1	–/–/–/–	Bow/Port/Starboard	5+
Light Battery	–/3/2/1	–/–/–/–	Stern/Port/Starboard	5+
Point Defense	4/–/–/–	–/–/–/–	All	–

Resadiye Class Battleship				
Class: Resadiye	Category: Battleship	Armor: 8	Operational Cost: 6	
Speed: 2–6	Altitude: 7	Turns: 1/45	Lift: 1	
Armament	**Firepower**	**Power**	**Fire Arc**	**Ammo**
Heavy Battery	–/7/5/3	–/+3/+2/+1	Bow/Port/Starboard	5+
Heavy Battery	–/3/2/1	–/+3/+2/+1	Stern/Port/Starboard	5+
Light Battery	–/4/2/–	–/–/–/–	Bow/Port/Starboard	5+
Point Defense	2/–/–/–	–/–/–/–	All	–

Barbaros Heyreddin Class Heavy Cruiser

Class: Barbaros Heyreddin	Category: Battleship	Armor: 8		Operational Cost: 6
Speed: 2–5	Altitude: 7	Turns: 1/45		Lift: 1
Armament	**Firepower**	**Power**	**Fire Arc**	**Ammo**
Heavy Battery	–/2/1/1	–/+4/+2/+1	Bow/Port/Starboard	5+
Heavy Battery	–/4/3/1	–/+3/+2/+1	Stern/Port/Starboard	5+
Medium Battery	–/3/2/–	–/+2/+1/–	Port	5+
Medium Battery	–/3/2/–	–/+2/+1/–	Starboard	5+
Light Battery	–/2/1/–	–/+1/–/–	Port	5+
Light Battery	–/2/1/–	–/+1/–/–	Starboard	5+
Point Defense	2/–/–/–	–/–/–/–	All	
Air Torpedo	2 (Speed 18)	+3	Bow	

Yavuz Sultan Selim Class Battlecruiser

Class: Yavuz Sultan	Category: Cruiser	Armor: 8		Operational Cost: 7
Speed: 2–6	Altitude: 9	Turns: 1/90		Lift: 1
Armament	**Firepower**	**Power**	**Fire Arc**	**Ammo**
Heavy Battery	–/5/3/1	2/+2/+1	Bow/Port/Starboard	5+
Heavy Battery	–/5/3/1	2/+2/+1	Stern/Port/Starboard	5+
Light Battery	–/4/3/–	–/–/–/–	Bow/Port/Starboard	5+
Light Battery	–/3/2/1	–/–/–/–	Stern/Port/Starboard	5+
Point Defense	2/–/–/–	–/–/–/–	All	–
Air Torpedo	1 (Speed 18)	+3	Bow/Stern	–
Air Torpedo	1 (Speed 18)	+2	Port/Starboard	–

Hamidiye Class Cruiser

Class: Hamidiye	Category: Cruiser	Armor: 7		Operational Cost: 4
Speed: 2–8	Altitude: 8	Turns: 2/45		Lift: 2
Armament	**Firepower**	**Power**	**Fire Arc**	**Ammo**
Medium Battery	–/2/2/1	–/+3/+2/+1	Bow/Port/Starboard	5+
Medium Battery	–/2/2/1	–/+3/+2/+1	Stern/Port/Starboard	5+
Light Battery	–/4/3/–	–/–/–/–	Port	5+
Light Battery	–/4/3/–	–/–/–/–	Starboard	5+
Point Defense	2/–/–/–	–/–/–/–	All	–
Air Torpedo	2 (Speed 18)	+3	Bow	–
Sky Mine	4 (Speed 6)	+2	Stern	–

Midilli Class Light Cruiser

Class: Midilli	Category: Crusier	Armor: 7		Operational Cost: 3
Speed: 2–8	Altitude: 9	Turns: 2/45		Lift: 2
Armament	**Firepower**	**Power**	**Fire Arc**	**Ammo**
Medium Battery	–/2/1/–	–/+2/+1/–	Bow/Port/Starboard	5+
Medium Battery	–/2/1/–	–/+2/+1/–	Bow/Port/Starboard	5+
Light Battery	–/3/2/–	–/–/–/–	Port	5+
Light Battery	–/3/2/–	–/–/–/–	Starboard	5+
Point Defense	2/–/–/–	–/–/–/–	All	–
Bombs	4 (Speed 6)	+1	Stern	–

Milliye Class Destroyer				
Class: Milliye	Category: Escort	Armor: 6	Operational Cost: 4	
Speed: 2–12	Altitude: 9	Turns: 1/90	Lift: 2	
Armament	**Firepower**	**Power**	**Fire Arc**	**Ammo**
Light Battery	–/2/1/–	–/–/–/–	Bow/Port/Starboard	5+
Point Defense	2/–/–/–	–/–/–/–	All	–
Choose one of the following:				
Air Torpedo	3 (Speed 18)	+2	Bow	–
Sky Mine	4 (Speed 6)	+2	Stern	–

Berk Efsan Class Torpedo Boat				
Class: Berk Efsan	Category: Escort	Armor: 4	Operational Cost: 8	
Speed: 2–14	Altitude: 9	Turns: 2/45	Lift: 3	
Armament	**Firepower**	**Power**	**Fire Arc**	**Ammo**
Point Defense	2/–/–/–	–/–/–/–	All	–
Air Torpedo	1 (Speed 18)	+2	Bow	–

Terrain

The discussion of terrain in a game of airships may seem a bit misleading. However, there are effects that impact airships trying to maneuver. In general, there are two types of terrain: ground and aerial.

Ground terrain consists of objects that are tall enough to impact the operation of an airship, features like mountain ranges, hills, etc.

Aerial terrain is in the air. The most common types are clouds, weather, and night conditions.

Ground Terrain

Most ground terrain has no impact on play. It is simply there to look pretty. However, some suitably tall terrain may reach above altitude band 0. This could be a mesa, large hill, or mountain.

Such suitably tall features can be assigned an altitude band. This is how high the feature reaches into the sky. If an airship comes into contact with this terrain and is at the same altitude band or lower, it is considered a collision with a larger vessel.

Aerial Terrain

Aerial terrain comes in these types: cloud banks, cloud cover, storms, and night.

Cloud Banks

A cloud bank is an isolated group of clouds. They typically cover no more than 25% of the board. For game purposes, a cloud bank is normally 6MU across in a generally circular shape, but multiple cloud banks can be combined into one big cloud bank. Each separate cloud bank has a random altitude band generated by rolling 1d6+2. The result is the altitude band of the cloud bank.

Cloud banks can be moved through with no penalties, but block line of sight.

Use the following rules for cloud banks:

- Cloud banks block line of sight. Shots can't be made through a cloud bank.
- Airships inside a cloud bank can't be fired on.
- Airships in a cloud bank can't fire out of it.
- If both airships are in the same cloud bank, they can only gain line of sight at short range. All shots are considered obscured.

Cloud Cover

Cloud cover assumes the entire board is covered by a layer of clouds. Randomly determine its altitude band by rolling 1d6+2. This is the altitude band of the cloud cover.

Airships at the same altitude band as the cloud are considered in the cloud cover and treated as if in a cloud bank.

Cloud cover can be moved through with no penalties, but it blocks line of sight. Use the rules for cloud banks, but assume the entire board is covered with clouds at the altitude determined.

Storms

Storms are similar to cloud cover. Follow the same rules, but below the cloud cover is a raging storm. Any airships under the cloud's altitude band are considered to be in the storm.

Airships in the storm are treated with the following rules:

- Line of sight is short range only.
- Command and Ammo test target numbers are increased by +1 (i.e. TN 4+ becomes TN 5+).
- Airships at the same altitude as the cloud band are treated as if they were in a cloud bank.

Night

An operation during the hours of darkness is a dangerous and harrowing experience. Night is assumed to impact all airships on the board. The following rules apply:

- All line of sight is short range only.
- Command tests target numbers are increased by +1, so (TN) 4+ becomes (TN) 5+.

Scenarios

The air navies of the various nations play an important role in the constant Great Power tension. Air navies are there to enforce the will of their governments on colonial interests. Over-aggressive captains and leaders can always be publicly reprimanded by higher authorities, providing plausible deniability. However, in such turbulent times small raids and border skirmishes can quickly escalate into short, brutal wars. However, the Great Powers are careful not to tip the balance too far. The maintenance of the status quo is far too important to be upset by something like a few hundred deaths.

The stability of the world order is critical to the economy, diplomacy, and industry. The Great Powers zealously protect the system. Even though they compete vigorously with each other, all players in the Great Power game understand that stability trumps any minor victory on the edge of empire.

Selecting a Scenario

There are a number of ways to choose a scenario for game play. Any mutually agreed-upon manner suffices. If needed, the method below can be used. It is optional and allows players to move onto the details of the game rapidly.

Outright warfare is frowned upon amongst the Great Powers and all fear a potential World War that could de-stabilize them all. However, low-intensity, semi-clandestine conflict is endemic in the system. This Scenario generation method is intended to reflect this truth.

Select Scenario

First, roll 1d6:

Roll	Scenario Type
1–5	Raid
6	Battle

Once you know if the game is a Raid or a Battle, roll 1d6 on the appropriate table below:

Raid Scenario Table	
Roll	**Scenario**
1	Raiders
2	Patrol
3	Mine the Airway
4	Bombardment
5	Blockade Run
6	Convoy

Battle Scenario Table	
Roll	**Scenario**
1	Surprise Attack
2	Aerial Assault
3	Escalation
4	Breakthrough
5-6	Fleet Action

Determine Attacker

Each Scenario is divided into attackers and defenders. This can be decided pre-game by any method. However, you may also dice for it. Roll a d6:

Roll	Attacker
1–3	Person who rolled
4–6	Person who did not roll

Determine Complications

Most battles don't take place in ideal conditions; they can break out at any time. To help show these complications roll 1d6 and consult the table below:

Complications Table	
Roll	**Complication**
1	Storm: the rules for a storm are in effect
2	Night Time: the rules for night time are in effect.
3–4	No complications
5	Cloud Cover: the rules for clouds covering the board are in effect.
6	Cloud Cover and Night Time: the rules for both night time and cloud cover are in effect.

Command Ship

Determine your command ship and Command rating for the fleet. The command ship must have the highest Armor value in the fleet. If multiple ships have the same Armor, you may choose which one is your command ship.

Setting Up Terrain

Set up terrain per the Scenario first.

If the scenario doesn't specify terrain, it is recommended that you place at least one item of terrain per 12MU x 12MU of table space. The attacker places one item of terrain anywhere on the board. The defender places the next item at least 6MU from the previous item. Continue alternating terrain placement until all terrain has been placed.

Determine an item's altitude when it is placed during placement. For example, you may specify a mountain reaches up to altitude Level 2. This may not apply to all terrain types.

Terrain Generator

If players wish, you can use this simple terrain table to generate the type of terrain. Before placing terrain roll 2d6:

Terrain Generator Table	
Roll	Terrain
2	Mountain (Up to altitude 4)
3–4	Mountain (Up to altitude 3)
5–6	Hills (altitude 1)
7–9	Land-based feature that does not impact play
10–11	Cloud Bank
12	2 Cloud Banks

Setting Up Your Fleet

Unless specified by the scenario, all fleets are deployed on opposite long table edges. They can be at any altitude and any speed when starting the game. They are deployed up to 6MU in from the table edge.

Players take alternating turns placing their ships with the attacker placing first. Alternate placing airships one at a time until all airships are placed. If one fleet runs out of airships to place, the other player simply places their remaining airships.

Advise your opponent of the Class, Altitude, Speed, and Armor of the vessel; for example: "This is a Bainbridge class escort at Altitude 5, going Speed 10, with Armor 6."

Scenarios

The following is a list of Raid and Battle scenarios. They are composed of the following details:

- Briefing: a high-level overview of the scenario and its objectives with some flavor text.
- Objectives: the goals of the battle.
- Forces: what warships both sides can bring to the table.
- Battle Sky: the rules for board set-up and deployment.
- Battle: rules related to the conduct of the scenario and winning conditions.

Victory Through Armor Loss

If a clear-cut winner for a scenario isn't determined by the end of the game, the winner is the side that inflicted the most damage on the other.

Add up the lost Armor points of all vessels of the force. Add 1 point for each critical damage. The side that inflicted the most damage is the winner.

Raiders

Briefing

Raiding is a fact of life on the edges of the Great Powers' empires. Airships attempt lightning-fast attacks on their local rivals to gain regional superiority. It is a matter of personal honor and career building for Captains, Commodores, and Admirals posted to these fringe areas. Such antics are tacitly encouraged by High Command, but a close watch is kept to avoid any potential escalation.

Objectives

The attacker is attempting to cripple as many enemy ships as possible, often targeting a specific one for destruction. Typically, this is the enemy command ship.

The defender is attempting to repel the attacker and minimize damage to their own fleet.

Forces

The attacker begins the game with a fleet worth up to 20 Operational Value. This can be made up of any combination of ships except battleships.

© Brigade Models

The defender begins the game with a fleet up to 25 Operational Value. This can be made up of any combination of ships, limited to a single battleship.

Battle Sky

Raiders can be played on any size board. However, a minimum area of 36MU x 36MU is recommended.

Determine attacker, complications, and terrain per the normal rules for setting up a game. Deploy as normal.

Ending

The battle lasts until all of one fleet's airships are Crippled, destroyed, have struck their colors, or at the end of 6 turns.

The winner is the fleet with non-crippled ships.

If both sides have non-crippled ships, determine the winner by Armor loss. Damage to the defender's command ship is worth double points.

Patrol

Briefing

The majority of an airship's service life is spent simply patrolling the airways, sea lanes, and borders of their own territory. Usually, these are boring and routine affairs. Sometimes, you run into the enemy. Sometimes, they are looking for a fight. Patrols are a necessary part of Great Power politics, keeping the other powers deterred from launching their own attacks.

Objectives

Each side is trying to cripple their foes and cause them to crash. Failing that, getting the enemy to strike their colors or withdraw are also acceptable.

Forces

Each side begins the battle with a fleet of up to 25 Operational Value. This can be made up of any combination of ships, but shouldn't have more than a single battleship. The difference in Operational Value shouldn't be greater than 4 points.

Battle Sky

The Patrol can be played on any size board. However, a minimum area of 36MU x 36MU is recommended.

Determine attacker, complications, and terrain per the normal rules for setting up a game. Deploy as normal.

Ending

The battle lasts until all of one fleet's airships are crippled, destroyed, have struck their colors, or at the end of 6 turns.

The force that still has non-crippled ships is the winner. Otherwise use Armor loss to determine the winner.

Mine the Airway

Briefing

Airships normally use tried and true routes between locations. These well-used flight paths carry commerce, passengers, and even warships between key locations. They are usually the fastest routes, with favorable winds and visibility. Their density of traffic makes them susceptible to active and passive measures to restrict access.

In this case, one Great Power has decided to send a strong message to a rival. They intend to block one of the key airways into their territory with sky mines. This is an aggressive act of diplomacy. It is also reckless, as it can quickly escalate into an act of war on the world stage. However, despite the risks, it is a popular way to raise the stakes in international relations.

Objectives

The attacker is trying to drop sky mines in a key portion of an airways into the rival power's territory. The defender is trying to stop them and keep the airway clear of sky mines.

The target zone is the area within 6MU of the center of the board. Roll 1d6+2. That is the altitude of the airway route to be blocked. The altitude bands immediately above and below it are included in the target area.

Forces

Each side begins the battle with ships that equal up to 25 Operational Value. This can be made up of any combination of ships, but shouldn't have more than a single battleship. The difference in Operational Value should never be greater than 4 points.

Battle Sky

The Mine the Airway scenario can be played on any size board. However, a minimum area of 36MU x 36MU is recommended.

Determine attacker, complications, and terrain per the normal rules for setting up a game. Deploy as normal.

Ending

The battle lasts until all of one fleet's airships are crippled, or at the end of 6 turns.

Calculate Armor loss to determine the winner. The defender loses 1 Armor point for each sky mine counter in the target zone.

Bombardment

Briefing

The Great Powers value territorial control, political power, military might, and economic dominance. Therefore, attacking targets that are symbols of these is a common feature of Great Power politics. One side's airships try to bombard and destroy a rival's assets to make a diplomatic point or for national prestige. Naturally, the rival power tries to stop them.

Objectives

The attacker is attempting to destroy a specific ground target. The defender is attempting to repel the attacker and protect their ground target.

Forces

Each side begins the battle with a fleet of up to 25 Operational Value. This can be made up of any combination of ships, but is limited to a single battleship. The difference in Operational Value shouldn't be greater than 4 points.

Battle Sky

The Bombardment can be played on any size board. However, a minimum of area 36MU x 36MU is recommended.

Determine attacker, complications, and terrain per the normal rules for setting up a game. The defender receives a ground target. It has the following profile:

Ground Target	Armor: 7

The defender places the ground target first, 12+d6MU from any board edge. The defender can place his fleet anywhere within 12MU of the ground target at any altitude, speed, and facing. Place one ship at a time, alternating with the attacker. The attacker's ships must be placed on the opposite board edge from the defender. They can be deployed anywhere on that edge up to 6MU in at any altitude, speed, and facing.

Ending

The battle lasts until the ground target is destroyed, or all attacking airships are crippled, destroyed, have struck their colors, or 6 turns.

If the ground target is destroyed the attacker wins. If not, the defender does.

Blockade Run

Briefing

One of the preferred tactics in Great Power politics is to place an economic embargo on key industrial areas of their rivals. This is frequently backed up by a blockade of airships to restrict merchant traffic. The natural response is to try and run the blockade to prove that it is ineffective. Normally, such tactics are short-lived, as other Powers negotiate a peace deal using the Concert of the World as a platform.

Objectives

The attacker is attempting to break the blockade and move their force off the defender's board edge. The defender is trying to repel the attacker and maintain the blockade.

Forces

The attacker is the blockade runner. They begin play with up to 20 Operational Value of vessels, no battleships may be taken.

The defender begins play with up to 25 Operational Value of vessels. They may have a single battleship.

Battle Sky

The Blockade Run can be played on any size board. However, a minimum area of 36MU x 36MU is recommended.

Determine attacker, complications, and terrain per the normal rules for setting up a game. Deploy as normal, with the following exception: the defender can be placed at any altitude and speed, but they can't face either the attacker or defender's board edge.

Ending

The battle lasts until a blockade runner escapes the board, or all attacking airships are crippled, destroyed, or have struck their colors, or 6 turns.

If a blockade runner escapes the attacker wins; if not, the defender does.

Convoy

Briefing

Trade is the lifeblood of empire. Therefore, supply lines and trade routes are ripe targets for rival Great Powers to attack. Over uninhabited tracts of land or over deep oceans, a convoy of airship transports is an easy target. To combat these attacks merchant vessels are accompanied by a military escort.

Objectives

The attacker wants to cripple or destroy as many merchant ships as possible. The defender is attempting to repel the attacker and keep the merchant ships alive and moving.

Forces

The attacker begins play with up to 20 Operational Value of vessels, but may not include battleships.

The defender is allowed to choose an equal Operational Value as the attacker, to a maximum of 20. They may have a maximum of 1 battleship.

The defender gets one free merchant ship for every 5 points of Operational Cost they take.

Battle Sky

The Convoy can be played on any size board. However, a minimum area of 36MU x 36MU is recommended.

Determine attacker, complications, and terrain per the normal rules for setting up a game.

Deploy as normal with the following exceptions: the defender places their merchant ships first. One merchant ship is placed in the center of the board at any altitude, speed, and facing. The rest of the merchants can be deployed anywhere within 12MU of the first.

Warships are placed in the normal way. Defenders must be placed within 12MU of the center of the board at any altitude, speed, and facing. Attackers can be deployed within 6MU of any board edge at any altitude, speed, and facing.

Merchants have the following profile:

Merchant	Command: 1	Armor: 4	
Speed: 0–6	Altitude: 7	Turns: 1/45	Lift: 1

Ending

The battle lasts until all merchants are crippled, sunk, or leave the board, or after 6 turns. If a ship leaves the board it is removed and can't return into play. It has escaped.

The attacker wins if they disable, destroy, or cripple all the merchant ships in the convoy. If this doesn't happen, calculate the winner based on Armor loss, including the merchant ships.

Surprise Attack

Briefing

Surprise is an important element of warfare. It allows one side to gain the upper hand and exploit it into a decisive victory. Typically, such an attack would try to catch enemy airships at anchor, resupplying, or refitting. Fleets are vigilant for raids, but with careful planning and execution, surprise can still be achieved.

Objectives

Each side is trying to cripple their foes and cause them to crash. Failing that, getting the enemy to strike their colors or withdraw is also acceptable.

Forces

Each side begins the battle with a fleet of more than 25 Operational Value. This can be made up of any class. The total number of Operational Value taken by both Powers should have a difference of less than 3.

Battle Sky

A Surprise Attack can be played on any size board. However, a minimum area of 48MU x 48MU is recommended.

Determine attacker, complications, and terrain per the normal rules for setting up a game.

The defender is placed first. They choose any board edge they wish and deploy in at least 6MU but no further than 12MU from the edge. All defenders are considered to be Landed. Since the defenders are surprised, they cannot activate airships until turn 2. Each defender must make a successful Command test (TN 4+). A success allows them to activate as normal. Once activated no further tests are needed.

The attacker is placed second. They are deployed up to 6MU of the opposite board edge in at any speed, altitude, and facing.

Ending

The battle lasts until all of one side's airships are crippled, destroyed, have struck their colors, or after 8 turns.

If both forces have ships that are still active, determine the winner by Armor loss.

Aerial Assault

Briefing

One Power is attempting an aerial assault, trying to land troops to capture territory they believe is rightfully theirs. Naturally, the enemy air navy is trying to stop them. This is a very aggressive move. Hopefully, a *fait accompli* allows the Concert of the World to restore peace, instead of allowing the attack to escalate into full blown war!

Objectives

The attackers are trying to land their troops within their designated landing zone. Every troop transport that successfully lands in the landing zone is assumed to disembark its troops. The defender is trying to stop the landings.

Forces

The attacker begins play with more than 25 Operational Value of vessels. This can be made up of any ships. The defender is allowed to choose roughly 3/4 the Operational Value of the attacker.

The attacker gets one free troop transport for every 8 points of Operational Value they take.

Battle Sky

An Aerial Assault can be played on any size board. However, a minimum area of 48MU x 48MU is recommended.

Determine attacker, complications, and terrain per the normal rules for setting up a game. Deploy as normal with the following exceptions:

The defender places the landing zone first. This is a 12MU x 12MU box placed 2d6+20MU in from the defender's board edge and 4d6MU from the board edge on the right side of the defender's deployment zone.

Once the deployment zone is on the board, both sides can deploy as normal.

Troop transports have the following profile:

Troop Transport	Command: 1	Armor: 4	
Speed: 0–6	Altitude: 7	Turns: 1/45	Lift: 1

Ending

The battle lasts until all troop transports are crippled, destroyed, have unloaded their troops, or the end of 8 turns.

The defender wins if no troop transports unload their troops.

Otherwise, roll 1d6 and add +1 for each troop transport that unloaded its soldiers. If the result is 7+ the Aerial Assault has succeeded, and the attacker is the winner. Otherwise, the defender wins.

Escalation

Briefing

If regional hostilities escalate picket airships are sent out to locate enemy air fleets. Once they have located the enemy, the pickets signal to their own fleet, who converge on the picket's location. As the battle escalates, airships continue to steam in and join the fight until a full-blown air battle has kicked off. This is known as an escalating engagement and is a danger to Great Power peace. Escalating conflicts can quickly turn into large scale war.

Objectives

Each side is trying to cripple their foes and cause them to crash. Failing that, getting the enemy to strike their colors or withdraw is also acceptable.

Forces

Each side begins the battle with fleets of more than 25 Operational Value. This can be made up of any ships. The total number of Operational Value taken should be within a 3-point difference.

They then select a picket force up to 15 Operational Value. This force should consist of escorts and cruisers only.

Battle Sky

Escalation can be played on any size board. However, a minimum area of 48MU x 48MU is recommended.

Determine attacker, complications, and terrain per the normal rules for setting up a game. Each player deploys their picket force as normal, up to 12MU in from the board edge at any altitude, speed, and facing. The remainder of the force is in reserve.

After the second turn, either player can attempt to activate a ship in reserve. To enter play the airship must make a successful Command test (TN 4+) in order to activate. A success allows them to activate as normal. Once activated no further tests are needed. The ship enters play anywhere on their board edge at any altitude, speed, and facing the player wishes.

Ending

The battle lasts until all of one fleet's airships are crippled, destroyed, have struck their colors, or after turn 8.

The force that still has active ships is the winner. If both forces still have active ships, determine the winner by Armor loss.

Breakthrough

Briefing

The purpose of an air navy is to prevent a rival force from pushing past it to attack targets within the Great Power's territory. Therefore, the attacker tries to bypass the defender, who is tasked with preventing them from doing so. Once past the defenders, the attacking ships can break up into roving packs and cause mayhem.

Objectives

The attacker is attempting to smash past the defenders and get into enemy territory to wreak havoc on soft targets. The defender must stop them from getting through by crippling or sinking them.

Forces

Each side begins the battle with fleets of more than 25 Operational Value. This can be made up of any ships. The total number of Operational Value taken should be within a 3-point difference.

Battle Sky

Breakthrough can be played on any size board. However, a minimum area of 48MU x 48MU is recommended.

Determine attacker, complications, and terrain per the normal rules for setting up a game. Deploy as normal with the following exception: The defender can be placed up to 24MU in from their board edge at any altitude, speed, and facing. The attacker can only be deployed up to 6MU in from their edge at any altitude, speed and facing.

Ending

The battle lasts until all of one fleet's airships are crippled, destroyed, have struck their colors, or after 8 turns. Ships that leave the board edge can't return to the battle.

The attacker wins if they get 25% of their starting Armor points off the defender's board edge. Otherwise, the defender wins.

© Brigade Models

Fleet Action

Briefing

A fleet action is the type of battle theorized by Admiral Alfred Thayer Mahan in his great work, The Influence of Seapower on History. His theories are still applied to the new mode of warfare. The goal of the two opposing fleets is to wipe the other from the skies and lay the enemy homeland bare for attack.

Objectives

Each side is trying to cripple their foes and cause them to crash. Failing that, getting the enemy to strike their colors or withdraw is acceptable.

Forces

Each side begins the battle with fleets of more than 25 Operational Value. This can be made up of any combination of ships. The total number of Operational Value between the two fleets should be less than 5.

Battle Sky

A Fleet Action can be played on any size board. However, a minimum area of 48MU x 48MU is recommended.

Determine attacker, complications, and terrain per the normal rules for setting up a game. Deploy as normal.

Ending

The battle lasts until all of one fleet's airships are crippled, destroyed, have struck their colors, or at the end of 8 turns.

The sole force that still has active ships is the winner. Otherwise, determine the winner by Armor loss.

Campaigns

The Great Powers are constantly at odds with each other over territory, policy, and prestige. Campaign plays pits two or more opposing Air Navies against each other in a battle for superiority in a particular theatre. These are typically small-scale skirmishes and personal struggles between officers in order to avoid such conflicts spreading and growing into a worldwide war.

Campaign Sizes

Before beginning a Campaign, all players should choose the size of the Campaign. This is the Operational Value that the Great Powers have allocated to that particular theatre of operations and to that commander.

The below are some guidelines:

- Small: 50 Operational Value.
- Medium: 75 Operational Value.
- Large: 100 Operational Value.

Pick a Campaign Fleet List

Each list is assumed to be a fleet under the player's command. Each player should create a list of all the ships in their Fleet up to the Operational Value allowed for the Campaign size.

The below are guidelines for each fleet:

- 50% must be spent on Cruisers or smaller ships.
- No more than 25% of the total can be spent on Battleships.
- Each ship must have a name, and each Captain must also have a name.
- One ship is designated the Flagship – typically this is the ship with the most Operational Value, but not always.

Strategic Assets

Once a fleet has been selected, it must roll for Strategic Assets. Strategic Assets are important locations that the Fleet is assigned to protect and support in their theatre of operations. These Strategic Assets will be where a Fleet can draw resources and supplies from in their theatre of operations. They are also tempting targets for attack.

Below are some guidelines for the use of Strategic Assets based on the size of the Campaign:

- Small: 3 Assets.
- Medium: 4 Assets.
- Large: 5 Assets.

At the start of a Campaign, each force is assigned a number of strategic assets based on the size of the Campaign (see above). A player can use Strategic Assets to do one of the following per Campaign Turn during the Determine Impacts Phase:

1. Repair 1 Armor or Critical Damage per turn.
2. Repair 1 airship of all damage, but the ship misses 1d3 Campaign Turns as it is repaired.
3. Earn an Airship 1d6 Experience but miss 1d3 Campaign turns.

© Brigade Models

4. Provide the re-roll of a single dice in the next Scenario.
5. Allow an extra 1 Armor Value of reinforcements.

Gaining Strategic Assets

The only way a Fleet can gain Strategic Assets is by taking them from other fleets. This can only be done by winning Scenarios. After winning a Scenario, both Air Fleets rolls their Flagships Command Dice + 1 dice for each of the factors below:

- Won the Scenario   +1 Dice
- Every 10 Armor Removed +1 Dice
- Sunk an Armor 8+ Ship   +1 Dice

Both factions are looking for a 4+ Target number. If the winning fleet scores twice as many successes as their enemy, they have managed to capture a single Strategic Asset of their choice from their opponent. Remove the Strategic Asset from the opponent's Fleet List and added it to the winner's Fleet List.

Going forward, the winner may use the new Strategic asset as they see fit in the determine Impacts Phase of the Campaign.

Campaign Turn

Campaigns run over a series of turns, similar to a game. Each Campaign Turn is broken down into a series of Phases. Each Campaign Turn will consist of the following Phases:

1. Determine Strategy
2. Determine Primary Enemy
3. Receive Orders
4. Determine Attacker/Defender
5. Pick Mission Force
6. Play Mission
7. Determine Impacts
8. Campaign Points
9. Check for End of Campaign

Determine Strategy

Each turn, the player determines the basic posture of his forces. Players choose to be either Offensive or Defensive This match up affects the types of scenario that will take place (see Receive Orders). Offensive is on the attack, while Defensive is protecting assets.

Determine Primary Enemy

If the campaign only has two players, this step can be skipped. If there are multiple players, you will then note which faction will be your primary enemy in this turn besides whether you are going to be Offensive/Defensive.

Receive Orders

As the Theatre Commander, you are provided a maddening series of orders from the Foreign Office, Secretary of War, Naval Command, and a multitude of other sources. It can be difficult for a local commander to determine the best course of action, and it is also what allows a local commander some degree of autonomy.

Reveal your Strategy and Primary Enemy at this time.

If two of you have listed each other as the Primary Enemy, you will only fight one air battle in the turn. This battle will be against your Primary Enemy, as both sides have focused their efforts on each other. If you and your Primary Enemy do not match, then you will randomly determine your opponent. This is based off the pool of players who chose you as their Primary Enemy. During a Campaign Turn each player may only fight each other a total of one time.

Once you have determined your Primary Enemy for the Turn, compare your Strategies and consult the table below:

Offensive/Offensive

One player rolls a d6 and consults the table below:

D6 Roll	Result
Offensive/Offensive Table	
1–2	Roll-up a Raid Scenario. The player rolling the dice is the Attacker.
3–4	Roll-up a Raid. The player rolling the dice is the Defender.
5	Roll up a Battle Scenario. The player rolling the dice is the Attacker.
6	Roll up a Battle Scenario. The player rolling the dice is the defender.

Offensive/Defensive

The Offensive player rolls a d6 and consults the table below:

D6 Roll	Result
Offensive/Defensive Table	
1–3	Roll-up a Raid Scenario. The player rolling is the Attacker.
4	Roll-up a Raid Scenario. The player rolling the dice is the Defender
5	Roll up a Battle Scenario. The player rolling the dice is the Attacker.
6	Roll up a Battle Scenario. The player rolling the dice is the defender.

Defensive/Defensive

One player rolls a d6 and consults the table below:

D6 Roll	Result
Defensive/Defensive Table	
1–3	Roll-up a Raid Scenario. The player rolling is the Attacker.
4–6	Roll-up a Raid Scenario. The player rolling the dice is the Defender

Pick Mission Force

Once the scenario has been determined, both sides choose the forces they will bring based on the scenario rules and requirements. An Air Ship cannot participate in more than a single battle in a Campaign Turn.

Play Mission

Play the scenario that was determined in the Orders Phase of the campaign.

Determine Impacts

Events within the battle will have impacts in the campaign. These fall into the following categories:

1. Permanent Damage
2. Experience

These are covered in more detail in the following rules (see pages 78 and 79).

Campaign Points

Allocate Campaign Points based on the results of the Scenario.

The winner earns one Campaign Point. If they inflict twice as many points worth of damage than they receive, it is a decisive Victory and they score two Campaign Points. If the difference is three times, then the winner earns three Campaign Points in a Massacre.

Check for Campaign End

Typically, a campaign ends when one player achieves a total seven Campaign Points. The winner must win by two Campaign Points or more. If they do not win by two, keep adding the points until one player exceeds seven and is ahead by two or more points

Once a player reaches seven Points, it triggers the "Final Battle" scenario. Players are encouraged to come up with a special scenario **or** the player with the highest points may choose a single Battle Scenario to play.

Spending Campaign Points

Besides being used to win a Campaign, a player may choose to cash in Campaign Points to perform special actions. Once spent, the Campaign Point is permanently lost. Only one action can be chosen per turn.

1. Call Reinforcements
2. Repair ships
3. Play a Special Missions

Call Reinforcements

The player cashes in a Campaign Points to earn up to 8 Operational Value of Reinforcements per one Campaign Point to their fleet. There is no limit to the number of Campaign Points spent in the end of the turn for Reinforcements.

© Brigade Models

Repair Ships

The player can cash in a Campaign Point to earn up to 8 Armor Value/Critical Hit repairs to allocate across his fleet anyway he sees fit. There is no limit to the number of Campaign Points spent in the end of the turn for Reinforcements.

Play a Special Mission

For one Campaign Point the player may choose the next scenario from the Raid types to be played in the campaign. The player can choose to be the Attacker of Defender.

For two Campaign Points the player can choose any Battle Scenario to be played next in the Campaign. The player can choose to be the Attacker or Defender.

Losing Ships

If a ship explodes or sinks during a game, it is assumed to be lost for the duration of the campaign. The wreck maybe recovered at a later date, but by the time it is repaired the Campaign is over.

Remove the ship from the Fleet List. It cannot be used in future Scenarios.

Permanent Damage

Many scenarios will end with ships damaged, with critical damage, and even crippled. If the ship did not sink or explode, it is still usable in the campaign.

At the end of any battle, a damaged ship may make a Command Check. Each score of a 4+ will allow the player to either add 1 point of Armor back to the ship **or** remove one Critical Damage effect.

The ship did not need to participate in the battle to make this roll. The ship cannot increase its Armor value higher than its initial starting point.

Experience

As vessels take part in engagements, their crews and captain will gain in confidence and skill. They will learn various tricks and stratagems to help them overcome their enemies. Vessels gain experience as they take part in engagements. When a warship has enough experience points, the ship will gain an advance. Typically, a ship will start with d6 experience points to represent their training, previous time in the air, etc.

Earning Experience

At the end of any scenarios, an Airship's crew will gain experience. The following is the criteria for gaining Experience.

Experience Table	
Criteria	Amount of Experience Gained
Survive the Battle	1
Inflict a Successful Hit	1
Cripple/Explode/Strike the Colors of an enemy Airship	1
Complete the Objective	3
Win the Scenario	1

An airship does not add any experience until after the Scenario is complete.

Experience Advances

As an Airship's crew gain experience they can earn an Experience Advance. An advance represents improved skill, ability, and tricks

The following table indicates when an Airship will receive an advance. This advance should be determined after the scenario has been completed and once the vessels Experience total meets the required threshold. This should be done with both players present in the engagement.

Experience Advance Table	
Experience Points	Advance
0–10	None
11–20	Level 1
21–30	Level 2
31–50	Level 3
51–70	Level 4
71–00	Level 5
101–130	Level 6
131+	Level 7

Advance Rolls

Once an Airship has achieved the threshold of Experience Points to achieve the next level, they can make a roll on the following table. Roll a 2d6.

Advance Roll Table	
2d6 Roll	**Result**
2	**Going Vertical:** The crew of the Airship has the Target Number reduced by 1 for all Command Checks made for an Emergency Climb Command. If the Target Number has been reduced to 2, re-roll the advance. A roll of a 1 is always a failure.
3	Airship Handling: The Airship has the Target Number reduced by 1 for all Command Checks involving Come About Command. If the Target Number has been reduced to 2, re-roll the advance. A roll of a 1 is always a failure.
4	**Jury-Rigging:** The crew of the Airship has the Target Number reduced by 1 for all Command Checks made for a Damage Control Command. If the Target Number has been reduced to 2, re-roll the advance. A roll of a 1 is always a failure.
5	**Marksmen:** The crew of the Airship has the Target Number reduced by 1 for all Command Checks made for a Fire for Effect Commands. If the Target Number has been reduced to 2, re-roll the advance. A roll of a 1 is always a failure.
6	**Veteran Airmen:** The crew of the Airship has the Target Number reduced by 1 for all Command Checks made for an Evasive Maneuvers Command. If the Target Number has been reduced to 2, re-roll the advance. A roll of a 1 is always a failure.
7	**Drilled Crew:** The crew of the Airship has the Target Number reduced by 1 for all Command Checks made for a Reload Command. If the Target Number has been reduced to 2, re-roll the advance. A roll of a 1 is always a failure.
8	Disciplined Crew: The crew of the Airship can make a Command Check to remove Friction markers in the End Phase during Friction Removal. Each roll of a 4+ allows 1 marker to be removed from that ship only.
9	**Stoke the Engines:** The crew of the Airship has the Target Number reduced by 1 for all Command Checks made for a Full Speed Ahead Command. If the Target Number has been reduced to 2, re-roll the advance. A roll of a 1 is always a failure.
10	**Blow Smoke:** The crew of the Airship has the Target Number reduced by 1 for all Command Checks made for a Smokescreen Command. If the Target Number has been reduced to 2, re-roll the advance. A roll of a 1 is always a failure.
11	**Dive, Dive, Dive!:** The crew of the Airship has the Target Number reduced by 1 for all Command Checks made for a Crash Dive Command. If the Target Number has been reduced to 2, re-roll the advance. A roll of a 1 is always a failure.
12	**Cross-Trained:** You may re-roll a single Command Dice on a Command check. The second result must be kept, even if it is worse than the original roll. You cannot have this advance more often than the Airship has Command Dice. Re-roll if the Air Ship does not have enough Command Dice.